My Perfect Gift

A Christmas Novella

E.J. SHORTALL

This is a work of fiction. Names, characters, places, brands, media, and incidents are either the product of the author's imagination or are used fictitiously.

MY PERFECT GIFT

ISBN: 0993297927
ISBN-13: 978-0-9932979-2-2

Edited by: Kim Sheard, Another View Editing
Cover designed by: E.J. Shortall, cover images courtesy of Depositphotos/dasha11, paulmaguire & sandralise
Inside graphics courtesy of Deposit photos/tpzijl & Barbra_Ford

Dedication

My Perfect Gift is dedicated to my dear
grandmother. I miss you all the time, but
especially at this time of year

Acknowledgments

It is always so hard, an almost impossible task, to thank and acknowledge everyone involved in helping with the publication of a book. From beta readers to bloggers, and everyone in between, it is the joint effort of everyone working together that gets our books into the hands of readers who crave their next fictional character fix.

Firstly I want to say a huge thank you to my lovely PA, Karen. You amaze, inspire and ground me on a daily basis. Without your loyal support and friendship I have no idea where I would be. I am so grateful you came into my life. You make this crazy journey bearable.

My thanks go out to the wonderful ladies of Shortall's Sexy Sirens, my amazing street team. Your support, encouragement and tireless pimping brings a smile to my face on a daily basis. Never underestimate how much each and every one of you means to me.

To my wonderful beta readers, Karen S, Nade, Brandi, Rhiannon, Karen P, Alison and Geraldine. Once again, thank you for taking the time to read through a rough draft and for embracing my characters as much as I did. Your encouraging words and statements of BBF love left me grinning from ear to ear. I feel blessed to have such an amazing group of critiques surrounding me.

There are an amazing bunch of authors otherwise known as the Indie Erogenous Zone (IEZ). Ladies you are my calm place in otherwise choppy waters. Thank you for your unwavering understanding, support and friendship. #IEZForever

Indies like myself rely on the mighty bloggers out there. I am forever grateful to each and every blog, individual and author who has shared details of my books and helped them get into the hands of the readers. There are just too many to individually name everyone but please know your support is truly appreciated.

To you, my wonderful readers. I don't think writing these things will ever get old. Writing my first 'acknowledgements' was amazing, writing my fourth is mind blowing. I started this journey not knowing whether I would sell a single copy. The fact that people not only purchased my books but then took the time to review and reach out never ceases to amaze me… and bring a huge smile to my face. So thank you, you are amazing.

Finally, I have to acknowledge and grovel to my hubby and our son, 'the child giant'. I know the ironing pile is kind of huge and the mountain of post looks like it's about to throw up around the house, so thank you. Thank you for understanding when I need to lock myself away to write. Thank you for listening to my frustrations when my characters will not conform and all I want to do is ditch them and give up. I love you and appreciate you both so much.

Chapter One

BLAKE SNOWDEN.

Lara Hollywell sat and stared at the bright yellow sticky note in her hands that held those two terrifying words.

What on earth do you buy the company vice-chairman as a Secret Santa gift?

The company she worked for, Turner-Mills Industries, employed over three hundred people. She could have had anybody's name but she had him. Blake. And for the first time since joining the company three years before, she didn't want him.

Over the years, Lara had fantasised about what she would love to give Blake, but it had never involved

1

shiny ribbons or bows. Though, carefully placing shiny bows over select parts of her anatomy wasn't a bad thought.

"So, who'd you get?" Sylvie asked excitedly pushing her way into the room and falling into one of the chairs opposite Lara's desk. "God, I love Secret Santa. The excitement, the suspense, wondering who's going to get back at someone for pissing them off."

Lara scrunched the paper into a tiny ball and dropped it into her wastepaper basket. She shrugged. "It wouldn't be a secret if I told you, would it?" she muttered, looking over the small, decorated Christmas tree on her desk at her excitable assistant.

"Spoil sport." Sylvie pouted then brightened, her painted red lips drawing up into a grin. "Guess who I got?"

Well it's certainly not Mr. I'm-gonna-be-difficult-to-buy-for Snowden, Lara thought. She hated Secret Santa, and always had. It was frustrating enough trying to come up with ideas for silly novelty gifts to give to people you didn't really know or like. It was going to be even worse trying to buy something for the boss she had been nursing a crush on.

Sylvie's eyes twinkled wickedly. "Billy in finance. We all know what he likes...." She made the universal gesture for oral pleasure by pressing her tongue into her cheek and pulsing her fist near her face. "I figured I'd go online and order him a deep-throat stroker."

Lara laughed. It had been a running joke all year that William 'Billy' Bevan had been caught with his pants down, receiving euphoric oral pleasure from one of the waitresses at the Christmas party the year before. Every couple of months, the photographic evidence would make its way around the office reminding everyone of his misdemeanour. How he had not filed some sort of harassment claim against certain members of staff amazed Lara. It was everybody's source of amusement, though, and Sylvie's gift idea would certainly cement Billy's encounter into the office's 'hall of shame'.

"You're t-terrible," Lara stammered through her giggles, which abruptly halted when her eyes wandered over to her office door. Standing there, looking sexy as hell, was her Secret Santa recipient himself.

At thirty-one years of age, Blake Snowden was the youngest vice chairman the company had ever had. He was also the hottest. His hair was in its usual unruly, yet sexy, dishevelment. His hazel eyes burned brightly behind thick, long lashes. A dark navy suit, with crisp white shirt and ruby-red tie, hugged every contour of his athletic body, while designer stubble gave him a sexy, bad boy look. He really was gorgeous.

Stop gaping. That's never going to happen, Lara reminded herself.

"What are you guys giggling about?" Blake asked in his rich, smooth voice. Leaning into the door frame, he crossed his arms over his chest. He was obviously settling in for the gossip.

Sylvie grinned. "I was just trying to get Bah Humbug here to spill the beans on whose name she got for Secret Santa. After all, as her little elf helper, I need to know if he or she is on the naughty or nice list. You see, I have this amazing talent for picking gifts I'm sure will please the recipient." At hearing Sylvie's statement, Lara's eyes shot from Blake to glare at her assistant.

There is no way I can enlist Sylvie's help, not for this, Lara thought. God only knew what Blake would end up with if Sylvie helped, and then, if he discovered who had bought the gift... no, it didn't bear thinking about.

"So, who did you get then? Anyone I know?" Blake asked.

If Lara wasn't mistaken there was a hint of amusement in Blake's voice. Did he know? No, he couldn't. Could he?

Lara aimed a pointed finger, first at Sylvie and then towards Blake. "Do I need to remind you two of the definition of secret? It means without the knowledge of others, a mystery. You know, a surprise." She looked at Blake who definitely had a knowing smirk on his handsome face. *Oh, God! How? How could he possibly know I drew him?* The pressure to find the perfect gift became even greater. She swallowed hard.

"I hate surprises," Sylvie grumbled, dragging herself from the chair. "I'll get it out of you, Scrooge. Mark my words. I will find out who you have!" Sylvie brushed passed Blake muttering about boring bosses and people with no festive spirit.

"Is she always that forward?" Entering the room, Blake strolled with easy confidence over to the seat Sylvie had vacated.

Lara watched him approach. Her eyes followed him as her knees trembled under her desk. When he unbuttoned his jacket before sitting down, she very nearly gasped. This was all too similar to a dream she regularly had. In her fantasy, they were in this very office, but it was she who was unbuttoning his jacket and slipping it off him before moving on to his shirt and tie, and then his trousers.... Things in the dream

4

didn't stop with Blake taking a seat and smirking at her like he was now.

She clenched her thighs together and moistened her dry lips.

Get a grip, Lara!

"So," Blake began, breaking the silence. "Secret Santa, huh? Not usually my thing, but I thought I'd play along this year. It should be interesting." He flicked at one of the small baubles on her tree.

I wonder what lucky person he drew, Lara thought. Knowing how particular he was about his job, she had no doubt that attention to detail would extend to the rest of his life. Whomever he had drawn would get a decent gift out of him, despite the limited budget. He was that kind of person, charitable, friendly, caring… She knew choosing the perfect gift for him would take time.

Blake struggled to repress his laugh. It was fun watching Lara squirm. He had jumped on the festive tradition this year as an opportunity to do something to try to win Lara over. After three years of watching from the side-lines, waiting for the perfect opportunity to prove to her he wasn't all work, work, work, with a side of playboy thrown in for good measure, Blake had finally decided to take the bull by the horns and… take part in Secret Santa. Or at least make it look like he was taking part in Secret Santa. Maybe he was just wimping out because he didn't want to admit he didn't have the courage to ask his head of marketing out on a date. Knowing that the names would be distributed this afternoon, he'd wanted to know if she had any idea who had drawn her name. Or rather, who had bribed Bernice, his assistant, to keep both their names out of the hat and forge the illusion of mystery.

The trouble was, he didn't have a clue what to get her. He was ashamed to admit, despite the regular business lunches and social functions they'd attended together, he knew very little about Lara. Yes, he could go for the universally accepted bottle of perfume or box of chocolates, but she didn't seem that type of person. From what he'd seen of her during meetings, he knew she was a strong character who would value something truly personal to her. He was going to have to do some research.

"Are you really not going to spill the beans on your Secret Santa?" His eyes lifted to meet hers.

"Tell you whose name I drew and ruin the spirit of the event? Never," Lara replied. He wanted to laugh at her obvious attempt to brush him off but knew he would just give himself away. The secret of this Santa had to stay well and truly buried.

How do I go about asking what she'd like?

"So, these things are supposed to be fun, right? Being the Ebenezer of the company up until now, I have no idea what people usually give each other in these things. If you were to receive the perfect gift from your Secret Santa, what would it be?"

Too damn obvious you idiot, Blake scolded himself.

He watched as Lara's cheeks flushed and her body gently convulsed, her teeth clamping onto her bottom lip. Maybe it wasn't such a silly question. Blake's blood heated and rushed downward, stopping in his groin and causing a painful bulge in his trousers. Was it possible Santa needed to visit an adult store to purchase her perfect gift? He was down for that - well, only if he got to help her enjoy the gift. He wished he knew what she was thinking.

"I, um…" Lara shifted in her seat and grabbed her glass of water, downing the entire thing in one go. "Now, that would depend entirely on who was buying." She cleared her throat and began fiddling with a pencil on her desk. "If it was from someone who didn't really know me, then I wouldn't expect anything more than a novelty chocolate figure or maybe a humorous mug. If it was someone I knew - somebody that knew me well - I would like to think a little bit of thought went into whatever it was."

Blake stared at Lara. That was it? That was all she was giving him?

"But there must be something you would like?" Blake pushed.

She shook her head. "Nope, I'm grateful for anything. I mean, isn't the spirit of Secret Santa supposed to be about the fun of giving, not about the receiving?"

Ah, so she is a giver, good to know.

"You're not giving much away."

She shrugged. "Not much to give. I don't have a wish list of things I expect. I'm not a conceited bitc… woman…" Blake grinned at her near miss. "I will gladly accept whatever is offered to me and will do my best to get a wonderful gift for my recipient. I would hope that he… or she, will also receive it with the spirit in which it is given." She looked Blake right in the eye as she said the last bit.

So, trying to get ideas from Lara herself wasn't going to be easy. Picking the perfect gift was going to be more difficult than Blake had first anticipated. He was going to need time... and maybe some divine intervention.

Moving carefully, so he could discretely readjust the swell in his boxers, Blake stood and strolled toward the door. "Well, it was nice chatting, Lara. I hope your Santa is kind to you."

At her desk, Sylvie had a radio on that was quietly playing Christmas songs. As Blake walked past, she was singing along as she read something on a piece of paper.

"What's that, Sylvie?" Blake enquired, pointing at the paper. It didn't look like anything business related.

"It's a flyer for the winter wonderland. I was just wondering what they had going on this year. Last year's was fantastic. I bought so many unique and unusual gifts there." She shrugged and placed the paper on the edge of her desk. "If I didn't already know what I planned on getting as my Secret Santa gift, I would be heading straight down there for ideas."

Blake glanced down at the glossy leaflet and noticed that it seemed to be advertising some sort of Christmas market. Realising it had the potential to provide a gift - or gifts - for Lara, he resolved to research it when he had the time and a little privacy.

Feeling a little more confident, and sure that his ruse had not been discovered, Blake shoved his hands in the pockets of his trousers and hummed The Twelve Days of Christmas all the way back to his office.

Chapter Two

LARA WONDERED WHAT the hell she was doing as she ambled through the rows of stalls set up in the park. She couldn't deny the place looked wonderful, and she was definitely getting the Christmas vibe with the coloured lights and festive songs playing everywhere. But she hadn't taken into account how cold it had become. Usually, at this time of year, she would be dashing from her front door to her car, her car to the office entrance, and then back again at the end of the day. She was never out in the crisp winter air long enough to really feel its bite. But as she strolled through the crowds shivering, she most definitely felt it.

It had been two days since Lara had seen Blake, two

days in which she had drawn a blank when it came to picking a gift for him. She'd spent most of her Saturday afternoon trawling online stores and auction sites looking for something he would appreciate and not just throw in a drawer and forget about. She chose to ignore the fact she wanted him to appreciate, maybe even love, her gift and then work out who it had come from so he could thank her in person.

And then laugh at you. She shrugged off the unhelpful thought and continued along the row, blowing into her hands every couple of minutes to try and warm them.

A brightly lit and decorated stall caught her eye and she ambled over, hugging her jacket tighter around her body. It seemed to be getting colder by the minute, and she wondered if they might soon get snow.

"I'll take this please," she said to the lady standing on the other side of the table. Lara held up a cute little angel trinket and handed it over. The woman was wearing a Santa hat decorated with tinsel and sleigh bells, and every time she nodded or shook her head, the bells tinkled a merry tune. Lara knew her grandmother would love it, being the self-confessed Mrs. Christmas trinket hoarder that she was. She smiled with fondness for her beloved nan, who embraced the winter holiday every year, making sure she brought the whole family together for lots of fun and laughter.

But at seventy four, her grandmother was no spring chicken, and Lara constantly worried she was overdoing things. She couldn't imagine a Christmas without Nan fiddling the Monopoly bank or guilting the family into wearing silly paper hats and reciting bad jokes from crackers.

Lara was thinking about her grandmother as she absent-mindedly fumbled around in her bag for her purse, not noticing the man standing beside her. Pulling the purse from her bag, she accidentally caught her work ID card too. As she lifted the purse, it fell to the ground. With a curse, she crouched down and used the glow of fairy lights to search for the dark lanyard and card. Spotting it near the leg of the table, she extended out her arm and brushed hands with someone also reaching for the item. She mumbled an apology and lifted her gaze, her eyes meeting luminous deep brown ones she couldn't help but know. Blake's presence startled her, and it took everything in her to not fall back on her arse on the cold, muddy ground.

"Blake, wha... what are you doing here?" she stuttered. *Why do I sound so breathy?*

"Probably the same thing you are." Blake handed Lara her ID and then offered his hand to help her stand.

"You shop in markets?" Lara couldn't believe it. "I assumed you'd be the type who'd get your assistant to do your shopping for you, or maybe rope in a personal shopper at a high end department store." She gave a gentle nod, pleased with her assessment.

"Why is it so unbelievable?"

Blake's tone was light and playful, but Lara detected a hint of hurt by the way his shoulders slouched and the small smile that had graced his lips fell away.

Shit! Did I hurt his feelings? Why do I always stick my foot in it?

Trying to hide her shame, Lara shrugged and turned back to the seller. "I don't know, sometimes you come across a bit arrogant."

"Sometimes?" His smile returned as he laughed.

"Okay, most of the time." She laughed too and handed cash over to the lady behind the table and waited while the ornament was wrapped in tissue paper.

With her purse, ID, and purchase safely stowed in her bag, she again looked at Blake. "So, what *are* you doing here?"

Blake grinned at her sheepishly, causing Lara to tilt her head to the side as she tried to understand his expression.

"What?" she asked.

"I'm hoping to get some inspiration for my Secret Santa gift." Blake grabbed her hand and started walking them through the crowds of people.

Taken by surprise, Lara cried, "Wait!" She planted her feet in the cold, damp grass and tugged her hand out of Blake's. "What are you doing?" She adjusted her jacket, trying to somehow get it to cover her a little more. It was definitely getting colder as the late afternoon light turned to dark.

Blake frowned, looking at her hand and then down at her thin trench coat. "Do you not have a warmer coat?" She shivered and shook her head, pulling her hands to her mouth again to blow warm air on them. "Gloves?"

"No."

"A scarf?"

"Nope."

"A hat?"

"Nein."

"Jesus, Lara. You must be bloody freezing." Blake reached around his neck and tugged off his grey scarf.

"Here." With a gentleness that surprised her, he began wrapping the scarf around Lara's neck, lifting her hair out of the way once he had secured it.

"Thank you," she whispered. It was such an unexpected, lovely, kind gesture, one she was most grateful for. The scarf was soft against her skin and smelled of Blake, a bold earthy scent mixed with a fresher laundry fragrance.

"You're welcome. You really should be wearing something warmer, Lara. You'll catch your death out here," he admonished her.

"I don't often come out in these temperatures," Lara countered with a bite. Who was he to scold her like she was an irritating child? "I don't need a thick woollen coat that I would hardly ever wear."

Blake's expression softened. "Sorry, I didn't mean to nag. I'm just worried about you. Here..." He wrapped an arm around her shoulder and pulled her in close. "Better?"

Lara couldn't speak. She was in the arms of Blake Snowden. How many times had she dreamed of being tucked up against him like this? How many fantasies had she had about being in this very situation? Yet she knew it meant nothing. He was just being a gentleman, concerned she'd end up with hypothermia or something. He was probably just worried about her missing work deadlines if she got ill.

When Blake had wandered into the crowds of people

at the market, he'd never expected to bump into the woman he'd been thinking about constantly for the last two days. She had invaded his every waking – and sleeping – thought. He'd tried fatiguing her out of his system by having a long hard workout at the gym. But after, he'd needed to shower, which meant he'd fantasised about Lara's hands stroking and caressing his body. The overwhelming feeling of desire he'd had for her in that moment led him to a powerful orgasm of his own making. He was ashamed to admit that jacking off to thoughts of Lara had been far more satisfying than many of his more recent sexual conquests. He had it bad for her.

Seeing Lara, with her bright eyes and cheeks flushed from the cold, had made the trip out in the freezing temperatures worth it. He hadn't known what to expect when he'd made the decision to see what the evening Winter Wonderland market had to offer. Sylvie's leaflet hadn't been too informative and what he'd found online was even less so. Still, he'd liked the concept of the market and other attractions, and with nothing other than his fantasies to keep him company, he had donned his thick woollen coat, scarf, and gloves and driven the five miles to the park.

And then, there she was, the object of his desire, crouching down at his feet looking utterly exquisite. He'd barely had any time to look for gifts, but seeing Lara had been gift enough - especially when he'd been able to orchestrate the opportunity to hold her.

It was nearing freezing temperatures, and all she was wearing was jeans with a flimsy, Burberry style trench coat. Admittedly, she was also wearing knee-high boots that did strange things to him, but still, she wasn't dressed for cold weather. He could feel her shivering as they wandered along the rows of stalls, looking at everything and nothing. He liked having her in his arms. It felt good, comfortable, and the caveman in him pounded his chest, claiming her as his possession to cherish.

It surprised him that Lara hadn't tried to escape his hold again. She'd certainly whipped her hand away quickly enough when he'd subconsciously taken it the first time. He'd felt like it was his natural right to do so—though she had made it clear it wasn't. She hadn't shown any signs before that his feelings for her might be reciprocated. In fact, she had gone out of her way to make it clear any relationship they developed over time was purely professional. So he savoured the feeling of her tucked into his side while it lasted.

They had been wandering along in silence for several minutes, both either content as they were or fearful to say something to break the moment. But Blake knew Lara was still cold, her trembling body was evidence enough.

"Let's get some hot chocolate," Blake murmured, turning his face into Lara's glossy hair. She had beautiful hair. It was long and brown, with a slight wave to it, and as soft as silk. It was hair he wanted to either stroke for comfort or wrap around his wrist as he carnally claimed her as his.

Taking one final covert inhalation of her heavenly scent, Blake started walking them toward a hot drinks stand.

"This place is wonderful!" Lara exclaimed happily. They sat on a bench set away from the crowds of festive bargain hunters, drinking steaming cups of sweet hot chocolate.

Whilst Lara sipped on her beverage and watched the people wandering past, Blake took the opportunity to study her. She really was stunning, in an understated way. *If only I could find her the perfect gift and convince her to be mine.* He was still no closer to deciding what to buy, and being so close to her was distracting him from his main purpose of being there in the first place. But maybe spending time with her out of work would give him some sort of inspiration.

"Have you never been here before?" Blake asked, needing something else to focus on.

Lara turned to face him, crossed her legs, and nestled her drink between her palms, absently stroking the label with her thumb. "No, this is the first time I've been to the market bit. Of course, I've been to a fair before..." Her expression fell for a moment as she blindly looked out at the park over Blake's shoulder.

Lara shrugged. "Some things just aren't meant to be."

Blake rubbed his neck. The emotion in Lara's voice screamed of unbearable sadness, and he found himself wondering where that melancholy stemmed from. Even more strongly, he wanted to take that sorrow away and bring the bright smile back to her face.

With a perfect aim, thanks to years of playing basketball at university, Blake shot his empty cup into a nearby rubbish bin and stood.

"Come," he said, reaching for Lara's hand.

"Where are we going?"

"We're going to go and relive our youth."

Chapter Three

LARA FELT LIKE a teenager as she strolled through the various rides and games booths with Blake. It had been years since she'd been to a fair - almost a decade in fact. The last time, she'd been at a well-known music festival with Devin, and he'd insisted he take her on the big wheel so she could see everything from a bird's-eye view. It had been a beautiful summer's evening, with a cloudless sky lit up by millions of stars above them and the sounds of rock music reaching them from below.

It had been at the top of that big wheel that he'd... She shook her head. *No I'm not going there, not tonight.*

That was in her past, and nothing could ever change what had happened. She knew she had to move on, it was just hard to actually do it.

Reacting to her hesitation, Blake gripped her hand tighter and steered them quickly toward a strongman game. As they stepped up to the machine, Lara could feel the energy and enthusiasm rolling off him. It was like being around a child on Christmas Eve.

"Watch this," Blake said, grinning over his shoulder as he grabbed the large wood and rubber mallet. "I bet you I can ring the bell in one hit."

"And if you don't?" Lara felt relieved that Blake was attempting to lighten the atmosphere between them. She hadn't meant to become so subdued but sometimes the memories became too much. Deciding to put it behind her for a while and just enjoy the moment, she smiled and joined in his merriment.

"If I don't then I'll..."

"Then you'll what?"

Blake narrowed his eyes as he appraised her. "It doesn't matter, because I'm going to do it. No forfeit will be necessary."

Lara chuckled as Blake turned back to the machine with a look of total focus on his face.

"What if I choose the penalty?" Lara asked, moving to Blake's side. Just then Blake swung the mallet high above his head, his eye briefly flicking in her direction.

The hammer came rushing down through the air and swung almost embarrassingly toward Blake's groin, totally missing its target.

"I win," Lara cheered, clapping her hands together.

"That does not count as a shot. You distracted me," Blake grumbled, scowling at the game.

"Yes it does, and no I didn't... well not deliberately... maybe just a little bit."

"You did it on purpose and you know it."

Lara watched on, giggling, as Blake sucked in a deep breath and lined up the mallet again.

"How about, if I do it, I get to kiss you?" he said without a glance in her direction. Lara gasped as Blake crashed the mallet down full force. The puck flew up the pole, leaving a trail of red and yellow lights in its wake. When it hit the top, a loud ringing sound echoed all around them, signalling Blake's victory.

With a triumphant grin on his face, Blake slowly turned to face her. "I do believe I won. Now, the question is, can I claim my prize?"

Her eyes widened. *I didn't agree, not to that.* Holding hands had been one thing. Even having his arm wrapped around her had seemed acceptable; she'd been able to reason that he'd been trying to keep her warm. But a kiss? No, that would be far too involved. A kiss suggested a level of intimacy she wasn't sure she was ready for. Even though her hormones were screaming at her that it was about time she saddled up and re-joined the race.

"I don't think that's a good idea, Blake," she said softly, hugging her jacket tightly around herself again.

"Oh, I think it is," he replied, smirking.

"No, Blake, it isn't."

His expression softened, morphing from playfulness to disappointment and finally settling on concern. "I'm sorry. I was only joking around."

Lara's gaze fell to the ground. Why did she have to be such a prude? Why couldn't she seize this opportunity and give in to her desires, just this once?

She knew why. Devin. She couldn't do that to him.

She felt Blake's eyes on her but couldn't look up. She was afraid of what he might see in hers if she did. She tugged her coat around her again, the temporary warmth she'd felt from her drink and being in Blake's presence had disappeared.

"Let's do something else." Blake broke the silence and placed a gentle, comforting hand on her elbow and encouraged her to walk with him.

As soon as she fell in beside him, he was walking with purpose, his face set and focused ahead. He seemed to be a man on a mission.

"Where are we going?" Lara chanced a glance in Blake's direction.

"On that," he replied, nodding his head forward.

Lara turned to look in the direction Blake had indicated and immediately stopped, once again planting her feet into the mud. "I... uh, I don't think so, Blake." She shook her head and started to walk in the opposite direction. There was no way she was going on that. She couldn't.

"Lara, wait! What's wrong?" Blake caught up with her in a few paces and stood before her, halting her escape.

"I'm not getting on that, Blake." She tugged on her coat again, trying to contain her shivers, only this time they weren't due to the bitter, cold air.

He placed comforting hands on her shoulders. "It's fine. You'll be safe."

"It's not that," she whispered.

"Then what is it?"

"It... it doesn't matter."

"Clearly it does. Are you afraid of heights?"

She shook her head.

"Do you suffer motion sickness?"

Again she shook her head.

"Please, Lara, whatever you are scared of, let me help you through it. Please, come and join me on the big wheel." He reached for her hand and she didn't pull away when his leather clad fingers entangled with her red, tingling flesh.

"You have nothing to be scared of," he said gently, with so much compassion she felt she might cry.

Peering over her shoulder at the illuminated, giant wheel, a flood of memories hit her. They were memories of years ago, of a happy time. But this was now. She realised she had to stop living in the past.

Blake squeezed her fingers in a reassuring gesture. She closed her eyes for a brief moment and let Devin's face fill her unseeing vision. She missed him, but there was no hope of him coming back. When she reopened her eyes, she looked at Blake and summoned a small smile, "Okay. Let's do this." She only hoped she wasn't opening herself up to emotions she thought she had long ago buried.

Blake walked cautiously over to the ticket booth. Was he pushing Lara into doing something she wasn't comfortable with? He didn't know her. Not really. Maybe she was acrophobic and was embarrassed to admit it. He sensed her sadness, though, and couldn't help but feel that maybe there was more to her wariness than met the eye. Before paying for the tickets, he stole another glance at her beautiful face. Whatever her reservations, he wanted to help her through them, and he wanted to bring back her smile. He also wanted an excuse to be cuddled up close to her, alone.

He handed over the cash and picked up their tokens, gesturing for Lara to precede him onto the ride. Once she was settled, he joined her on the narrow seat and secured the metal bar in place. Blake grabbed Lara's hand and waited for the ride to start. *Please let this be the right thing to do. I really don't want to end up upsetting and hurting her so she ends up pulling away.*

As the ride's mechanisms slowly rotated them up and around, Lara's gaze stayed fixed dead ahead. She was shaking, and Blake could even see the sharp rise and fall of her chest as she tried to control her breathing. He fully expected her to shout out at any moment, declaring she wanted to get off.

They hadn't spoken a word to each other the whole time it took to get to the top. Blake scrambled for something to say to break the silence and hopefully ease Lara's tension.

He didn't need to think for long because suddenly, from below, he heard shouting and the slowly revolving ride jerked to a stop. Peering over the edge, Blake saw a group of youths causing a scene and arguing with the wheel's operator.

"Oh God," Lara moaned beside him. She was gripping the rail with white knuckled force.

Without thinking, Blake instinctively slid closer to her and wrapped a protective arm around Lara's shoulder.

"I'm sorry, Lara. You should have said you were afraid of heights. I would never have brought you on here," he whispered against her hair, feeling guilty beyond belief.

Shaking her head, she replied timidly, "It's not that."

The ruckus continued below and the pod began swaying slightly in the frigid, night time breeze. Blake began stroking his fingers up and down her upper arm, trying to soothe her.

"What is it, Lara? You can tell me. I promise I won't judge." He hoped his tone carried the truth of his words. He wanted her to trust him. He wanted her to feel comfortable enough with him to open up.

Lara remained silent for a moment before she took a shuddering breath. "I thought I might be able to do this," she whispered. "I thought time might heal the wounds, but it never does. Not really. Being up here just rips the scab off again."

Blake had no idea what she was talking about. "What wounds?" he asked softly.

Lara took another deep breath and hiccupped as she tried to maintain some level of composure. Her eyes closed and her chin dropped. Blake could see the sorrow etched into her soft pale features. "Being up here, it brings back memories, memories of a happy time."

She opened her eyes and stared out at the dark night sky. "The last time I came on a big wheel, I was with Devin. We were at a big, well-known music festival, somewhere we went every year. We both love… loved music. It was how we met. We'd been at a concert and he'd been pushed into me. He'd tipped almost a whole bottle of beer over my new jumper." A small smile tugged on her lips.

"We got to talking and discovered we had a lot in common. We were inseparable after that."

Blake continued stroking along her arm, allowing Lara all the time she needed to gather her thoughts and tell her story.

"Every year, we went back to that same festival. On our third visit, just before the headliners came on, he pulled me over to the fair and onto the big wheel. I tried to protest, I didn't want to miss the band, but he just smiled, kissed my head and led me onto the ride anyway.

"I thought something was odd when we were the only ones on the ride, but I just put it down to everyone else having the sense to be in the field watching the gig." She turned her head and gazed out as though transported back to that moment in time.

"Devin was silent the whole way up. And with each passing second, he began fidgeting, like he was scared... or nervous. When we finally reached the top and the wheel stopped, the view was incredible. I was speechless. At first I was a bit pissed off because I wanted to be down with everyone else, singing and dancing. I couldn't really see why we were up there, despite the amazing view. But then, after a couple of songs, he shifted in his seat so he was facing me and pulled a box out of his jacket pocket. Right there, on top of that big wheel, watching our favourite band singing live, he asked me to marry him." A sob escaped her and she pulled a clenched fist to her mouth as though trying to hold it back. But a lone tear betrayed her by sliding down her cheek.

"Two weeks later, he shipped out to Afghanistan. I never saw him again." She said the last on a strangled whisper.

Tears were now falling down her cheeks, and Blake couldn't bear it any longer. He wrapped his other arm around her and pulled her in tight, hugging her into his chest. Over the top of her head, Blake looked out at the comings and goings of the fair and wondered how anyone could survive that. He'd never been in love that deeply before, had never even been close to asking someone to commit their life to him, but he knew to have loved and lost in that way must have destroyed her.

"I'm sorry," he whispered against her hair as she sobbed into his chest. It felt stupid, a clichéd saying that someone used when they didn't know what else to say. And that was the thing; he didn't know what to say. All he could do was hold her and try to soothe away her sadness.

As the wheel began turning again, Lara pulled back and swiped at her eyes with the sleeve of her coat. "I'm sorry," she mumbled. "I didn't mean to become a blubbering wreck."

Blake smiled at her sadly and ran his thumbs across her cheeks. "Please don't apologise. Not about that."

The pod reached the bottom again with Blake staring into Lara's eyes. He knew in that moment that his feelings for her were so much deeper than he had ever expected. He knew he would move heaven and earth to prevent Lara from ever experiencing that kind of pain again. The only problem was, she wasn't his to protect.

Chapter Four

LARA COULDN'T GET off the ride quick enough. As soon as the pod stopped and the safety bar was lifted, she scrambled out of the seat, determined to put as much distance as possible between her and Blake.

I can't believe I spilled my guts like that. I made a total fool of myself.

The rubber soles of her boots squeaked on the metal steps as she rushed away from him. It was time to go. Never in all the years since she'd received the phone call that had shattered her heart—her whole world—had she broken down in front of someone like that.

Devin had been her life. From almost the moment she'd met him, she'd loved him unconditionally. She'd trusted and believed in him and supported his decision to join the army. She'd always known there was a risk something could happen to him when he left, but she'd put it to the back of her mind, preferring to live in blissful ignorance than face what could have been something soul-destroying. And when it happened, it was.

Lara had lived in a cloud of numbness and despair for eighteen months after Devin died—killed by a rebel force attack whilst on patrol in Helmand. Seven years later—she hardly ever spoke of him. It hurt too much. Yes, she'd moved on. Yes, she had eventually learned to try out new relationships. But she always held back, prevented herself from taking things too far, for fear of betraying Devin's memory and because of the absolute terror that she might just end up caring for someone only to lose them too.

Not talking about him, not recalling those feelings, was how she'd coped. So, having opened up to Blake like she had, her mind swirled in a vortex of mixed emotions and memories. She had felt so comfortable in Blake's arms, talking so freely to him about something she had barely even spoken to her family about. The whole evening confused her.

She needed distance. Space in which to regain her composure and lock that painful time back in the ice box it had laid dormant in for several years.

"Lara, wait!" Blake caught up with her before she'd even managed to make it a few metres from the ride. He wrapped his long fingers around her elbow and gently tugged so she turned to face him. When her eyes met his, it was there, just as it always was when people learned of her loss. Pity. She didn't want to see that look on his face. She didn't ever want to see that look on anyone's face. Despite her broken soul, she had learned to become the strong, independent, and successful woman she was. She didn't need pity, just some understanding and the space to move on with life at her pace.

"I'm sorry, Blake, but I need to go. It's getting late." She jerked free of Blake's grip and stared at him, willing him to understand how she felt.

Blake frowned and opened his mouth to speak but stopped. It was clear he wanted to say something, or ask something, but instead he simply nodded as if defeated.

Lara suddenly felt awkward. She'd been having a wonderful time with Blake, enjoying the sights, sounds, and smells of the market and fair with him. They'd talked and laughed like they were old friends, and he was so attentive and caring. It was clear not all the rumours about him were true. He did have a heart, and a kind one at that. Maybe at a different time or in a different life she would have tried to act on some of her fantasies about him. As it was, she would just have to admire him from afar.

Reaching out, Lara placed a gentle hand against Blake's cheek. His skin was warm under her fingers, and the bristle of his two-day-old beard prickled against her cold flesh. "Thank you," she said in a hushed tone. "Thank you for listening and for a lovely evening."

With a small, apologetic smile, Lara withdrew her hand and stepped away.

She had barely stepped a few paces before Blake was once again at her side, placing a comforting hand on the small of her back as he steered her toward the market stalls. "Let me walk you to your car."

They walked through the crowds of jolly revellers in a relatively comfortable silence. Lara was sure Blake thought she was nothing more than an overemotional wreck. She certainly still felt embarrassed about her outburst.

At the candy floss stall, Blake stopped and peered over at her with childish delight in his eyes. "Before we go, it would be rude not to, right?" He jutted his head in the direction of the giant, stainless steel bowl of fluffy pink sugar. Before Lara could reply, he'd handed over a few pound coins to a middle-aged lady with greying hair and a giant mole on her chin. Lara stood fascinated as the woman attempted to pull off a flirtatious smile. She was reminded of the evil stepmother in the pantomime she had taken her niece to see just the week before. *Oh no you don't!* Lara felt like childishly calling out in a sing song voice. She had to quickly turn around and stifle her giggle before either Blake or the candy floss lady caught on to her silliness.

When she managed to get her grin under control, she turned around and found Blake watching her, his eyes shining with amusement and an eyebrow cocked. Looking over his shoulder at the lady now stirring the bowl as if stirring a witch's cauldron, Lara couldn't help it. "She's behind you," she blurted out in a fit of giggles. Grabbing the stick of intricately sugared cotton webbing, she skipped off, her mood suddenly lifting.

Blake shook his head, smiling. He'd felt her pulling away from him, returning to whatever dark place she'd been in since her fiancé died. When she'd run off the ride, he'd seen pain and even embarrassment on her face. Why, he wasn't sure. She had nothing to be embarrassed about. As they'd walked back through the fair, he had wracked his brain for something to do or say that would help ease the growing tension between them.

That's when he'd spotted the candy floss stand.

As a child, he remembered his grandfather buying him a stick of floss to cheer him up when he'd failed to win a goldfish on the hook-a-duck game. He'd been so excited by the candy that he'd managed to make a right sticky mess and had even found candy floss stuck in his hair. By the time he'd finished it, that goldfish had been long forgotten.

At the very least, Blake had hoped that buying a stick of the confection would give him a little more time with her. As it turned out, it gave him more than time; it brought a beautiful smile back to Lara's face and a playfulness he'd not yet seen from her. Both of which he liked. A lot.

"Oh my God, this is so good yet so bad," Lara moaned as she pulled off another strip and allowed it to melt on her tongue.

Part of him was beginning to regret his purchase because the noises she was making were starting to cause his jeans to feel a little tight and uncomfortable in the groin area.

"Give me that," he barked playfully, as he snatched the stick from Lara's hand. Maybe if he held the candy, she would stop making those noises long enough for him to get back in control of himself.

"Give me that back."

"What's it worth?"

Lara stopped walking and pouted. "Would you really deny a woman her sugar fix?"

He laughed. "Absolutely not. I know it's more than my meagre life is worth."

Pulling some off, he offered it to Lara. She eyed him suspiciously then reached out, but before she could take it, he pulled it back and pushed it into his own mouth. Moaning at his own greedy pleasure, he kept his gaze locked on Lara's.

She narrowed her eyes. "Oh you want to play games, huh? Do you not know anything, Mr. Snowden? Women do not play fair when it comes to sweets."

Blake laughed again as she tried to sneakily grab the stick from his grasp.

"Is that so?"

"Uh huh," she replied. Blake was captivated by Lara's intent expression as she persistently grabbed for the candy floss. She was quick, but he was quicker, and every time he would snatch it out of the way before she could get her hands on it.

"Blake!" she whined, eventually getting bored with his game.

"Okay, okay," he chuckled, and handed her what was left. "You really like candy floss that much huh?"

She shrugged. "It's okay. It is a bit sickly but

something that has to be done at the fair. If there's one thing I hate though, it's losing." With a wink she tugged off some more and popped it into her mouth.

"Me too," he mumbled, watching again as she poked out her tongue to lick her lips.

Blake and Lara slowly made their way back through the market and along the pathway to the parking lot. They had chatted like old friends, discussing work, music, TV and family. Neither of them had done any more shopping, but they had learned more about each other. Blake discovered that Lara, like him, was one of four siblings. She had two older brothers and a younger sister, while Blake had three older brothers. One of those, Blane, worked as a site supervisor for Turner-Mills. He also learned that he and Lara were practically the same age. Only four months separated them, with Blake being the elder. The more he uncovered about her, the more he wanted to know and he found his attraction to her growing.

Finally, they stopped beside Lara's car, a Chilli Red Mini Cooper. She hit her remote and the car beeped to life. "Thank you again, Blake. Despite... well, you know... I've had a great evening. I guess I'd better be going." She smiled and reached for the handle.

"Lara, I..." Blake felt like Lara was slipping away from him. If he didn't do something or say something, she would be gone. Their time together would become a distant memory and they'd go back to being casual work acquaintances.

He cleared his throat, but then, like a shy teenager, he couldn't think of anything to say. He felt like he was a character in a cheesy Rom Com.

"Goodnight, Blake."

"Lara, wait." She turned to face him again, her bright smile clouded with a hint of annoyance. "You've... um." He reached out and gently swiped his thumb across her lower lip. "You had candy floss on you."

Her cheeks reddened as her eyelids lowered. She was embarrassed. It was such a charming expression on her. "Thank you."

"You're welcome," he whispered.

Blake do something you idiot. Let her know you're interested.

Realising it was now or never, he gently cupped her cheek, rubbing soothing circles over her chilled flesh. The moment her gaze met his, she knew his intentions. It was clear through the widening of her eyes and the slight falter in her breathing. He gave her a moment to pull away, and when she didn't, he leaned in, wrapping his other arm around her waist, and pressed his lips gently to hers. It wasn't a long, smouldering kiss, but when he pulled back, Blake felt as though his whole world had just shifted into a new dimension. He'd had a taste and wanted more. So much more.

Blake closed his eyes and rested his forehead against Lara's. She hadn't spoken but she also hadn't slapped him or stormed off. As a first kiss, Blake thought it had gone well.

"Are you okay?" he asked on a hushed breath.

"Yes," she replied almost hesitantly. "Blake, I..."

Fearing she was about to brush him off and spoil the moment, he placed a soft kiss to her hair and stepped back. "It's okay, Lara. No need to say anything. I'll see you at work tomorrow?" He offered her a genuine smile and began walking backwards, unwilling to turn away from her, just as snow started falling from the sky.

Lara looked dazed and absolutely stunning with snowflakes resting on her hair and eyelashes. "Yes," she replied. Then, as if she'd been freed from a trance, she blinked and shook her head. "Blake, wait!" she yelled as he turned to head to his car. "Your scarf."

"Keep it," he called out over his shoulder. She needed it more than he did.

"But…"

"Think of it as a gift." He turned just long enough to see her lift the scarf to her nose. The dreamy look that spread across her face as she inhaled gave him hope. If only Blake could help Lara past her demons, he would do anything to prove he was the right man for her.

Chapter Five

LARA FELT LIKE a stalker freak as she yet again sniffed the scarf wrapped around her neck. It still smelled like Blake.

She'd spent the night curled up in bed with the soft grey wool, savouring Blake's scent, recalling the evening they'd shared. At first, she'd tossed and turned, but eventually she'd drifted into a fitful sleep.

In the morning, she'd awoken feeling surprisingly energised and eager to get her day under way. Her favourite blush pink shift dress and jacket were pulled from their hangers and she paid extra attention when pulling her hair up into an elegant knot and applying her make-up. Despite her inner turmoil, she needed the comfort that came from looking good. There was also the possibility that she might just run in to Blake.

It doesn't matter, Lara. He's a work colleague, possibly a friend. It can never be anything more, she tried telling herself. With a final look in the hallway mirror, she grabbed her keys and bag and left to start her busy day.

"It's all junk, junk, and more junk... Oh, and the flyers for Chesterton Mews came in, *finally*." Sylvie strolled in to Lara's office flicking through a pile of post. "Whoa! What's with the dreamy look, Ms. Bossman? Spill the beans." Lara rolled her eyes as Sylvie dropped the post on her desk and eagerly settled into her usual chair.

"I don't know what you're talking about." But, of course, she did. She'd been staring at Blake's scarf, hanging on the coat rack by the door, daydreaming about their kiss for the past hour. It had been quite some time since she'd last had a man's lips on hers, and despite having enjoyed the feeling, it confused her emotions too.

Sylvie scoffed and rolled her eyes. "Of course you don't. You usually walk around here looking like Brad Pitt accosted you during the night... So, who is he?"

Lara gave her assistant her best *you are getting nothing from me* smile and remained silent. Well, there wasn't exactly much to tell.

"You are such a meanie. You know I tell you everything," Sylvie whined.

Lara snorted. She loved her assistant. Sylvie was fun, loyal, and super-efficient, but you couldn't tell her anything unless you wanted it broadcast via Sylvie FM. There was no way Lara was going to admit the fact that she secretly had the hots for the company vice chairman and that he'd kissed her the night before.

They bantered back and forth for a few minutes. Eventually, Sylvie gave up trying to get the scoop from her boss and returned to the safer topics of the day's schedule. They needed to prepare for the press release for an exciting new development the company was building in Cheshire.

"Knock, knock. Am I disturbing anything?" At the sound of the deep, slightly gravelly voice, Lara peered up from her notebook and blushed. In the doorway, as he had been a few days previous, stood Blake. Wearing a well-fitted, black pinstripe suit with pale grey shirt and a deeper charcoal grey tie, he looked his usual powerful, yet beautiful, self. She couldn't contain the smile that lit up her face.

"Mr. Snowden. Twice in one week, aren't we the lucky ones! If I didn't know better I'd think you have a thing for my boss here," Sylvie said looking at Blake. The corners of her mouth twitched into the semblance of a grin.

Blake didn't even blink, but Lara felt the heat rise even further in her cheeks.

"Actually, come to think of it..." Sylvie looked from Blake to Lara and then back again. "Hmm, I wonder." She had a mischievous, knowing glint in her eyes, and Lara knew that at some point Sylvie would be hounding her again for information.

"This reminds me," Sylvie said. "Have you thought anymore about your Secret Santa gift?" Sylvie returned her attention to her boss. "You don't have much time left to get it. I can help if you want. I just need to know who you have."

Lara chortled. "Not going to happen, Sylvie."

"Fine." Sylvie stood and walked toward the door. "Have it your way." She stood in front of Blake for a moment, giving him the once over with eagle eyes before making her way out to her desk.

Lara got an eerie feeling of deja vu when Blake sank down into the chair Sylvie had vacated. At any moment, she expected him to start talking about gifts and Santa. But whatever his reasons for being there, she was pleased to see him.

Blake leaned in, and with his elbow on the desk, he rested his chin on his palm. "So, Lara."

She grinned, it was an instinctive reaction. "So, Blake."

"I had a great time last night."

Lara's gaze shot to her doorway, wondering if Sylvie was out there eavesdropping. "I did too." She contemplated getting up to close the door, but knew that would probably only add fuel to Sylvie's already inquisitive fire.

"Then I think we should do it again... spend time together that is, not necessarily at the fair. I mean, that was great and all, but I-" Blake rambled, nervously tracing along the edge of the desk with his fingers.

"Blake?"

"Yeah?"

"I get the picture."

He chuckled and grinned at her, seeming a little embarrassed. "What are you doing Saturday? Maybe we could go out for a meal or something."

Was he seriously asking her out again? The thought both thrilled and terrified her. But it didn't matter, she already had plans. "I'm sorry, I can't. I'm busy Saturday."

Blake's smile dropped. "Oh, that's a shame, maybe another time?"

She thought about it for a moment. *It's decision time, Lara. Become the mad, old cat lady or take a chance on living your life again. Why not go out and have some fun?*

"I'm taking my niece ice skating at three on Saturday afternoon, but I would love to maybe meet up some other time," she said smiling. *There, that wasn't so hard.*

Blake's smile reappeared, lighting up his face. It was clear he was thrilled with her decision to give him a chance.

Lara studied him for a moment. She was mesmerised by the way his eyes sparkled under the fluorescent lighting in her office, and how his Adam's apple bobbed up and down when he asked her questions about her skating experience. She absent-mindedly mumbled replies, lost in her thoughts and memories of the previous evening.

"Lara?"

She snapped out of the trance she'd fallen in and peered at Blake shyly. "Sorry, I was just…" She trailed off, embarrassed at having been caught daydreaming, even if it was about the man sitting in front of her.

Blake grinned at her knowingly. "Look, I have to be in a meeting in five minutes but I'll be in contact soon to arrange that date." He stood and buttoned his suit jacket, keeping his gaze locked on hers for any sign that she might change her mind. Then he was gone, striding out of her office with his usual confident grace.

"Interesting!" Sylvie shouted, rolling her chair back

so she could poke her head through the door, grinning.

Lara laughed and threw a pen at her. "Shut up!"

"Little Miss Can-be-uptight-but-I-love-her-anyway is getting all sassy and loved up on me, huh?" Sylvie picked the pen up, winked at Lara, and then returned to her desk.

Lara slumped back in her chair with a sigh. Maybe 'loved up' wasn't quite the right term for how she was feeling, but around Blake, she certainly felt more alive than she had for quite some time.

The last time Blake had gone ice skating he'd been about thirteen. He'd fallen over, hurt his backside and his ego, and hadn't dared to try it since. However, on hearing Lara's plans, a sneaky idea began to manifest in his head.

"Bernice, could you see if you can book me two tickets for the outdoor ice skating rink for Saturday, three p.m.?" Blake's assistant blinked up in surprise as her boss breezed past. Blake wasn't usually one for using his assistant for personal matters, but this was urgent. He needed those tickets. Now if only he could convince Caitlyn to go with him.

Blake looked at his watch; he was going to be so late for his meeting. "Oh come on, Caitlyn, you know you want to. I'll make it worth your while." He sounded desperate and he knew it.

"What's it worth?"

"I'll buy you a Barbie or something."

Caitlyn laughed. She actually laughed at him. "Oh my God, Uncle Blake, what am I, five or something?"

Blake ran a hand through his hair. How was he going to convince his niece to go along? He needed her to agree. He couldn't just show up at the rink; that would look desperate. *But you are desperate,* he inwardly reminded himself. "Look, Caity, I need you to do this for me. Please! I'll get you anything you want, just please let me take you ice-skating."

"Who is she?" His niece asked bluntly.

"Who's who?"

Caitlyn sighed and he could picture her dramatically rolling her eyes just like his sister did. She was so much like her. "Uncle Blake, I'm twelve not ninety and senile. I know when love's involved."

"I don't love her," he blurted out. But saying it made him realise that it wasn't true. Of course he loved her, or at least cared deeply for her. He'd done so since she'd made him hard when she'd given him a dressing down one day in a meeting about two years ago. He had been royally pissed off with her at the time but also thoroughly impressed with her feisty, no-nonsense, let's-get-this-done attitude. He'd desired her ever since but had never realised how deep those feelings for her had become.

"Yeah, and pigs might fly. I'll have to come now just to see who it is that has you so worked up. What is it mum always says about you... oh that's right... 'He'll never get a woman. Nobody in their right mind would put up with him.'"

"She says that?" He was wounded.

She giggled. "Yep, all the time. So when are you picking me up?" Caitlyn sounded far too cheerful, and Blake began questioning the wisdom of asking her along. Maybe it wasn't such a smart move after all. His niece could be cunning when she wanted to be.

Ending the call, he prayed this would not backfire on him.

Blake buttoned his jacket and stepped out of his office on his way to his meeting.

"Two three p.m. tickets all booked and paid for Mr. Snowden," Bernice said with a grin as Blake passed her.

"Thanks, Bernice."

Blake could only hope that Lara didn't think he was some weird stalker when he turned up at the ice rink.

Chapter Six

"LARA, WHERE ARE you? We have important business to attend to."

Lara smiled at her grandmother's impatient tone. It was their annual Christmas preparation committee meeting. The committee consisted of Lara's Nan, mother, younger sister Deborah, and one of her sisters-in-law, Heidi. It was the same every year. They would sit at Nan's dining table with too sweet tea and discuss who would be there for Christmas, who would bring what with them – which was the same every year, and then Nan would start nagging Lara about her love life, or lack thereof. Lara was the only one of her siblings still unmarried, and Nan made it perfectly clear she would not be happy until her granddaughter was loved and well looked after.

Lara switched her phone to her other ear and tugged her bag onto her shoulder. "I'm just leaving work now, Nan. Do you need me to bring anything in with me?"

"Just yourself, Lara, dear. Although walking in with a handsome young man on your arm would make an old lady happy."

Lara laughed. "I'll be there as soon as I can, Nan. See you soon." She hung up, shaking her head. She had learned long ago to laugh off Nan's nagging ways. She knew Nan only had her best interests at heart. Her grandmother just wanted her happy and settled down, with the two point four children and nice house in a respectable neighbourhood that she'd always dreamed of. Of course, that dream had been in reach, until Devin was taken from her.

As she pushed through the heavy glass doors and out into the dark car park, her smile had dropped. Even now, so many years later, she could not help the feelings of sadness that always washed over her whenever she thought of Devin. She pondered whether she would always be that way.

"You really should get a warmer coat you know. You'll catch your death out here in these temperatures." Blake emerged from the building just behind Lara, pulling on a pair of black leather gloves. He stopped next to her, watching her with a 'pleased to see you' grin.

She looked down at her coat, the same coat she'd been wearing the night before. "I'll be fine. My car's only over there." She pointed to her car, which was now sporting a light covering of snow.

Blake looked at the car then frowned. "Here, take this." He shrugged out of his coat and held it out to Lara.

Shaking her head, she said, "Oh no, Blake, no. I couldn't take your coat. You'll be the one catching your death if I do."

"We'll both be catching something if we stand around here arguing about it. I won't take no for an answer." He placed the coat, warm from being wrapped around his body, over her shoulders. "Come, I'll walk you to your car."

Blake slowly led her across the snow covered tarmac, being careful so she didn't slip or trip in her heels. When they reached the car, he told her to get in and start warming it while he cleared the snow for her. She couldn't ever remember a guy offering to clear her car for her. Without gloves, the task of snow scraping was always a painful one, so she gratefully accepted his offer and climbed in, but not before insisting he take his coat back.

Five minutes later, the car's interior was warm and Lara was absently singing along to Mariah Carey's "All I Want For Christmas Is You." She started at the sound of knocking on her window. Blake stood there with reddened cheeks and a silly grin on his face. She hit the button to lower the window. "I didn't know you could sing."

Lara's own cheeks flushed. "Um, yeah. I wouldn't really call that singing, cat wailing maybe."

He chuckled and leaned in, gripping the top of the lowered glass. "Nah, you sounded great from what I could hear. Anyway, it's all done. Do you have far to drive? It's bound to be slippery out there."

"No, I've been summoned to my grandmother's for operation Christmas get-together. She lives just up the road, near the rectory."

Blake nodded and stepped back. "Okay, but still take it easy. I'd hate for anything to happen to you." He tapped the roof of the car as he stepped away.

Lara sat for a moment, watching Blake walk away. She hadn't even said 'Thank you.' He'd just done one of the sweetest things anyone had ever done for her, and she hadn't had the courtesy to show her appreciation. As Blake climbed into his car, Lara sighed and put her Mini in gear. A moment later, she was crawling slowly along the snow covered roads in deep thought.

When she pulled up outside her Nan's place twenty minutes later, thanks to the snow slowing her down, she had realised she cared quite deeply for Blake. She'd wondered, during her drive, if maybe something could happen between them. He did seem to be interested in her after all. Then she'd nearly crashed when thinking of Devin had brought wetness to her eyes and obscured the changing traffic light. One thing was for sure, she had stronger feelings for Blake than she'd originally thought. She didn't just have a youthful crush over a good looking guy, but she still didn't know if she could ever act on those feelings either.

Lara opened Nan's front door and stepped inside. It smelled like home. Lara had spent so many happy times there growing up. Returning always managed to ease her tensions whenever she was feeling off kilter. She brushed the snow off her hair and hung up her coat before making her way down the wide hallway and into the kitchen where she could hear female voices.

"Oh, look she's here. Come take a seat, sweetheart, you look tired." Lara's grandmother jumped out of her seat for a hug and then gestured for her to take a seat next to her mother. "I'll make you some tea. How was work?"

"Same old, same old," Lara replied, pulling out the chair. "I can't wait for the break. It has been long overdue."

Nan placed a floral print china cup and saucer in front of her. "You work too hard." She patted Lara on the shoulder and retook her seat across the table.

"It's all part and parcel of the position, Nan. The work won't do itself."

Nan lifted her cup to her lips. "Yes, but how do you expect to meet a nice young gentleman if you are working all the time."

Lara felt a kick beneath the table and turned to see her sister barely containing her laughter. Debbie had always joked that she'd deliberately reeled her husband in at a young age so she would never find herself on the end of her grandmother's nagging, matchmaking ways.

"She'll find someone when the time is right."

Lara gave her mother a grateful look.

"She doesn't have time to wait around for Mr. Right to drop into her lap. I would love for that sexy, Superman guy to fly in and sweep her off to make beautiful babies…"

"Mother!" Lara's mother gasped as Debbie and Heidi chuckled.

"I don't have the time to wait. I'm not getting any younger." There it was, the veiled attempt at a guilt trip. Nan had an uncanny knack for making Lara feel guilty for the simplest of things.

"I'm not ready, Nan," she mumbled. "Maybe one day I will be."

Her mum placed a comforting hand over hers. "Lara's still grieving."

"Poppycock. She needs to move on. Devin has been gone for years," Nan said, her thin lips drawing in.

Lara sat in stunned silence as everyone around the table decided to speak about her love life as though she were no longer there. She sipped her tea, wishing she was still in her office talking to Blake.

"Oh my," Nan suddenly screeched, making the room go silent. "She already has someone."

Lara's cup landed on the saucer with a loud crash. She met her grandmother's gaze. "What? No, I don't. That's absurd."

"Oh, don't try the denial thing with me, missy. You know I have a sixth sense about these things."

It was true. Nan had told Heidi she was pregnant with Daisy before Heidi had even considered it a possibility. She'd also warned Devin about going on that tour, she'd had a bad feeling about it. Lara shivered at the thought.

"So who is he?"

Lara clasped her shaking hands together on her lap. "There is nobody, Nan. I promise."

"But you like somebody, don't you!" Lara felt all eyes in the room on her.

"Maybe, I'm not sure," she whispered.

"Why are you not sure sweetheart?" This time it was her mother who spoke.

"It's too soon." Tears stung the backs of her eyes.

Nan moved up behind her and kissed the back of her head. "It isn't too soon. He's been gone seven years... It's okay to be afraid and fearful. But, Lara, you need to have faith that there is someone out there who will make you happy beyond your wildest expectations. What if this man is him? You need to open your heart and let someone else in."

Lara closed her eyes. "I don't know how." She had never admitted that to anyone, not even herself.

"Lara, you cannot live your life like that. You're not like that with your work, so why be like that with love?"

"Because it hurts so much more when it is all taken from you," she whispered.

Two hours later, Lara threw her bag onto her kitchen counter and headed to the fridge for a glass of wine. Her family had been relentless in their advice giving. In the end, with very little Christmas planning done, she'd feigned tiredness and made her excuses.

She barely knew how she'd made it home in one piece when, for the whole journey, all she'd seen was Devin and Blake dancing around in her mind.

Her phone chirped with an incoming text. Pulling the phone from her bag, she found a message from Blake.

Please tell me you made it home ok. I've been worried about you.

Surprised by his almost intimate contact, she quickly typed out a message saying she was fine and thanking him for his earlier help.

Kicking off her shoes, she curled up into the corner of her plush, L shaped sofa and sipped her wine. She tried to put order to her rampant thoughts but nothing was working. With a sigh she threw her head back against the cushions and stared up at the ceiling. *"What is wrong with you?"* she chastised herself.

She moved her gaze to the small table at the end of the sofa and stared at the image of Devin's face smiling at her. "Jesus, Dev, what should I do? I miss you so much, but I'm lonely. How can I move on? How could I ever possibly love somebody else like I loved you?" Tightness spread across her chest as she struggled to contain her emotions. Christmas was always the hardest, the one time of the year she missed him most. It was when she wished more than ever to have him back home so she could be cuddled in his strong, comforting arms. *Without you here, Christmas just isn't the same anymore.* She would never, could never, forget him. He had been her life. But maybe it was time to start a new one. She didn't know if she had love in her again, but she thought that maybe she could at least learn to care deeply for somebody else. Maybe she already did. As Lara drifted off to sleep, she dreamed of snow, fairgrounds, Blake, and a handsome soldier telling her it was time to let go and find happiness with someone new.

Chapter Seven

BLAKE PULLED HIS car into a parking spot and switched off the engine. His niece had been like a fly buzzing around his ear the whole journey, nagging him for details about his new girlfriend. His sister hadn't been much better when he'd gone to pick Caitlyn up. She'd fired a hundred questions at him, wanting to know more about Lara than he was able or willing to tell.

They followed the signs to the ice rink, with Caitlyn jabbering on about the latest movie she wanted to go to see and what she'd been doing in school. Blake had one focus, find Lara.

He hadn't seen much of her all week. Back to back meetings and tight deadlines had meant either being away from the office or stuck behind his desk. They had managed a couple of friendly text conversations but those had been short and trivial. They'd also crossed paths in the corridor once or twice, but Blake had always been rushing off to his next appointment.

Now that he was out of the office, his number one focus had become spending time with Lara. He wanted her to see the real him and he hoped joining her on the ice would give him that opportunity. The thing was, she still had no idea he would be there.

"Oh my God, Uncle Blake, look there's Daisy. She's in my class at school." Caitlyn shook his arm excitedly. He was sat on a bench, putting on his skates, and the sharp movement made his grip on the boot fastener slip. He cursed under his breath. *Why are these things so difficult to do up?* He was already second guessing his decision to be there and he hadn't even stepped foot on the ice.

With the boots finally securely fastened, he looked at his niece. "That's great, Caity. Just don't leave me looking like an idiot on my own while you go off whizzing around with a friend, alright?"

She was looking over his shoulder with a huge grin on her face. "I don't know about the idiot thing, but I doubt you'll be on your own."

Before he had a chance at a comeback, someone was standing beside him. "Blake, what are you doing here?"

Once again, Caitlyn and Daisy sped past them on the ice, laughing at Blake gripping the side wall like it was his lifeline. His face was scrunched in concentration as he tried desperately to coordinate his feet to move forward without falling. The girls both looked like they had been born to skate, moving fluidly around the ice without any hint of fear at all.

If he was nothing else in life, Blake was determined, and he was determined he would not fall flat on his backside and humiliate himself now. His niece would never let him hear the end of it if he did. Plus, there was the matter of male pride. He didn't want to look like a complete idiot next to the graceful beauty who was patiently moving along beside him.

"You know, Blake, you'd probably find it a lot easier if you loosened up a bit." Lara's voice held a little quiver from trying to contain her laugh. He looked up quickly, just long enough to catch her smile, and then returned his gaze to his skates. If he could see them, and they were still on the ice, then he was okay. It meant he was still in an upright position.

"Stop looking down, you're making it worse," Lara chastised him. "Here." She stepped in front of him, stopped moving, and reached for his hand, encouraging him to let go of the wall.

"Um, Lara, I don't think that's a good idea." It was too late. She'd grasped both his hands in hers and had begun to slowly move backwards, pulling him along with her.

"You wanted to skate, Blake. Pulling yourself around the edge is not skating."

He watched her face as they slowly moved across the ice. She looked so relaxed and carefree for a change. It was a good look for her. He wanted to see her smile like that more often. "So how come you are so good at this? You and Daisy look like pros while I look like a drunken fool trying to fumble his way home."

She threw her head back and laughed. "You do not look like a drunken fool, just someone who hasn't skated before. Believe me, we see it every year. I used to skate quite a bit when I was younger. When Daisy was old enough, and they started putting up this annual winter rink, I began bringing her along. As you can see, she has no fear of the ice whatsoever." She looked sideways as her niece passed by in an elegant flurry of backward crossovers followed by a spiral that had Blake's eyes watering from the sheer speed of it. "This has become our Christmas tradition."

"So can you do those tricks too?" He found himself incredibly turned on by the thought of Lara wearing a tight sequinned outfit. He could almost picture her elegantly floating around the ice performing a flawless routine.

Oblivious to Blake's musings, Lara told him about the lessons she'd had when she was a child and of the few trophies she'd won. He was so caught up in her enthusiastic dialogue, he didn't even realise when she let go of one hand and they moved across the ice side by side.

But when they next reached the far corner of the rink, Blake needed to stop for a moment. His ankles and knees were beginning to ache. None of the girls were showing any sign of pain, and he didn't want to admit it, but he was definitely getting sore. "And I thought I kept myself in shape," he grumbled.

"It's not about being fit or in shape. You're using muscles you don't normally use in your regular workouts. Those are the ones that are protesting." That was an understatement. Blake couldn't wait to get out of the skates and back into his comfortable trainers. Daisy and Caitlyn whizzed past, calling out a challenge to Lara as they went by. Not wanting to be outdone by a couple of pre-teens, Lara winked at him once before she sped off after them. Blake watched her, laughing and smiling as she chased the girls and then had a mini dance off with Daisy, causing a crowd to gather around and cheer them on.

In that moment, Blake knew he was a goner. She was it for him. She was beautiful, intelligent, caring, the list was endless.

"Penny for 'em," Lara said, laughing as she skated back to Blake. He hadn't realised he'd been so obviously daydreaming.

"I was just enjoying your little dance show out there-"

"Omph." Lara was suddenly in his arms. Blake instinctively wrapped protective arms around her, pulling her tight into his chest. A group of boisterous lads had sped past behind her and knocked her forward.

"Are you okay?" He scowled at the boys who were now being chased by the ice marshals.

"I'm fine," she mumbled into his coat. Blake relaxed slightly when she didn't try to escape his hold. He liked having her in his arms. A quick glance over the ice showed the girls were still happily skating around.

"Those boys shouldn't be allowed on the ice. They could have seriously hurt you," he said softly against her hair.

"Blake I'm fine. They are just being young lads."
She pulled back and looked him in the eye. "Honestly,
no harm done."

He wasn't convinced. His heart was still pounding
from the overwhelming desire to go and teach the
young thugs a lesson. "Are you finished? I don't think
I could go around once more if you paid me."

"Yeah, our time is up soon anyway."

Blake grabbed her hand and surprised them both by
skating smoothly to the doorway in the board walls.
He wanted her off the ice where it was safe.

Blake and Lara wandered along, watching and laughing
as Daisy and Caitlyn played in the snow that had
started to fall again, adding more to the already
blanketed ground and trees. Occasionally, the girls
would whisper to each other, giggle, and then pelt the
adults with snowballs. Blake and Lara gave back as
good as they got, working as a team to bombard their
nieces. What should have been a short walk turned
into an hour of frolicking around.

Eventually, when everyone was cold and wet, the
girls spotted the hot chocolate stand and demanded a
drink before they went home. Blake didn't hesitate; it
allowed him more time with Lara.

With cups in their hands, they slowly meandered
their way back toward their cars. Blake hadn't been
able to forget the brief kiss he'd given her the last time
they had left this place. Her lips had been so soft and
inviting, and though the girls would prevent another
kiss this time, he'd love nothing more than a repeat
performance. *Next time it'll last a little longer,* he thought
to himself.

The girls skipped on ahead happily, talking animatedly about their favourite boy band hit or celebrity crush. Blake was thrilled they were getting along so well. Other than with family and a couple of close friends, his niece was usually quiet and reserved. He hoped maybe this little excursion had been as beneficial for Caitlyn as it had been for him in terms of building friendships... or relationships.

Lara slipped one hand inside her pocket and took a sip of her drink. "So, you never explained what you were doing here today, Blake. You didn't say anything about coming when I mentioned it the other day."

He'd hoped she wouldn't ask that. He didn't know what to say that wouldn't make him sound like a stalker. It would have been better if she'd just assumed it was a happy coincidence. He met her gaze and began to come clean. "To be honest, Lara, I-"

Lara suddenly squealed so loud a nearby dog started barking. Daisy had thrown a snowball. Only, instead of it hitting her aunt, it had connected with the large evergreen tree they were currently standing beside. The impact had caused an avalanche, covering Lara in snow and ice. "Oh my God!" she yelled. "That is so bloody cold."

Blake tried, he really did, to contain his laugh, but with Lara looking like a sexy snow-woman he couldn't help himself. His face broke out in a broad grin, and the deep rumbles of his laugh soon followed. She glared at him as she desperately swiped at the snow melting on her clothing and tried to get the cold intrusion out from under her top.

"I'm sorry," he tittered. "It was kind of funny though."

"Maybe it was for you."

Blake stepped in closer. He was now mere inches from her and could see how vivid her eyes were, how warm and inviting. Lifting his hand to her hair, he smoothed away the snow that had remained glistening like millions of tiny stars.

"Are you okay?" he asked softly.

She shivered but nodded. "I'm fine, just cold. Maybe I need to take your advice and buy myself a nice, thick coat." Her teeth began to chatter as another piece of ice slid down the collar of her jumper.

"I couldn't agree more." He twirled a lock of her hair around his finger, surprised by its softness beneath his fingers. "I would hate for you to get ill or something."

Blake just ask her you idiot.

"Lara, I-"

"Blake, I'm sorry, but I need to get home, I'm so cold."

Disappointment and frustration swamped him. "Of course. We need to get you out of those clothes." Lara's brows shot up in surprise. "Um, I mean you need to change your clothes, you know, into something warm and dry."

Blake couldn't understand why he was suddenly stammering like a pubescent lad trying to entice a girl out on a first date. All he wanted to do was ask her out to dinner some time. Of course, he hoped that one time would lead to many more times.

Seeing Lara shivering in front of him, Blake's protective alter ego surfaced. He unzipped his black bomber jacket and shrugged out of it. "Here, put this on." He reached out to wrap it around her shoulders, but she tried to wriggle away, arguing that she didn't need it. Blake was nothing if not a determined and persistent man, though, and he was resolute.

She finally conceded defeat as Blake managed to help her slip the coat on. "Blake, haven't we been here before? You'll be the one getting cold and ill now." He grinned when she tried to conceal the fact she was snuggling against the faux fur collar.

"I'll be fine. It's only a short walk back, and I wasn't the one who got covered in snow." He chuckled again as the image of Lara getting buried by the white stuff replayed in his mind.

They made their way back to the cars with Lara murmuring the occasional gripe about silly egotistical men who would not listen. He simply grinned and winked at her.

When they reached their cars, Blake knew he had to seize the moment and ask her out to dinner. He didn't know when he'd next get the chance. They'd had the perfect afternoon, and he wanted that to continue.

"Lara, I-"

"Aunt Lara, can you call mum and ask if Caitlyn can come round please." Blake growled under his breath in frustration when Daisy inadvertently blocked his chance to speak.

Whilst Lara spoke with her niece, Blake looked to the heavens and prayed for a break. All he needed was thirty seconds of uninterrupted time so he could make his move.

After a quick discussion, and phone calls to both sets of parents, it was agreed that Caitlyn would go to Daisy's for the evening. As the girls piled into the back of Lara's car, Blake joined her on the driver's side.

"After you've dropped the girls off, will you join me for dinner?" he asked suddenly, before he got interrupted again, or lost his nerve, or the apocalypse began.

Lara froze. "I'm sorry, Blake. I can't." She turned and removed his coat. With a sad smile, she handed it over. "I've had a wonderful time this afternoon, but I'm not ready for anything else just yet. Please try to understand."

Blake took the coat from her and watched in stunned silence as she climbed into her car and drove away.

What now? He thought to himself as he pulled his coat back on and zipped it up. It smelled faintly of Lara, of the subtle soft floral fragrance she wore. She had buried herself deep under his skin and she didn't even realise. Walking towards his own car, he wondered if she would ever come around.

Sitting behind his wheel, he stared out at the falling snow, remembering the short but exhilarating time they'd spent together. *You need to get her the perfect gift, Blake. Prove to her how much she means to you. Show her you care.*

As he drove away, a million thoughts for gifts swam through his mind, but none of them came close to being perfect for Lara.

Chapter Eight

HEIDI OPENED THE door and greeted the two girls who rushed past her. Lara tittered remembering herself at that age. They were obviously in a hurry to escape to Daisy's room.

"So, who is he?" Heidi asked with a grin as she leaned back against the wall. Lara shook the snow off her boots and stepped inside.

"Who's who?"

"You know who I'm talking about, Lara. *The* guy. The guy you were at the rink with. The guy I could hear in the background when you phoned."

"Oh that's—" She was cut off by Caitlyn who had stopped at the top of the stairs and peeked her head over the banister.

"That's my uncle, Blake, Lara's new boyfriend." The girls ran off leaving Heidi gaping at Lara.

"Boyfriend?" Heidi choked out.

Lara cowered under the pressure of her sister-in-law's stare. "It's a long story. I'll explain another time. Caitlyn's mum will be by later to pick her up." She hoped distraction would be the best form of defence against over inquisitive prying.

Lara hung her coat on a hook hoping Heidi would drop it. "Nice try but you're not switching the subject on me. I want all the deets." She rolled her eyes. *No such luck.*

Five minutes later, Lara found herself sitting at her sister-in-law's small kitchen table, sipping on a cup of tea and telling her everything about Blake.

"He's the one isn't he? He's the one Nan was talking about!" Heidi stated matter of factly.

Lara cringed, recalling her grandmother's apparent sixth sense. If Nan was right, Blake would be Lara's Mr. Right, even though her grandmother had never even met him.

"Nan doesn't know what she's talking about." Lara sipped on her tea and tried to ignore Heidi's deep, penetrating gaze. She wished, just once, her family would stop interfering in her love life.

Blake stood in the corner of the large boardroom, wondering what all the fuss was about. It was just Secret Santa. Presents had been purchased and wrapped; now they just needed to be exchanged.

He had been in a terrible mood ever since Lara had knocked him back and bruised his ego. He understood her reticence, he really did, but it wasn't like he was getting down on one knee and proposing marriage. One dinner date, that's all he'd wanted… to start with anyway.

"And there I was thinking Lara here was the Bah Humbug of the company. Cheer up, Ebenezer, it's Christmas!" Sylvie said, strolling past him and swaying her hips in time to some jazzed up version of a classic Christmas song.

Lara stopped beside him and laughed awkwardly. "I'm glad she's passing that particular baton onto you. It was kind of getting old and worn."

Blake had to hold himself back from reaching out and pulling her into an embrace. It was becoming harder and harder to be around her now that he understood the depth of his feelings for her. All week, he'd managed to stay away from her. He'd steered clear of the staff rest room, stayed late locked up in his office in case he ran into her when leaving, and when they'd been in a meeting together, he'd deliberately avoided eye contact and got the hell out of there as soon as he could. He knew he should just talk to her and tell her how he truly felt, but he was worried she would just reject him again.

"Blake, this is yours," Sylvie shouted from across the room, holding up a nicely wrapped gold parcel with a big red bow. Of course, he already knew who it was from.

"You do know the story of Scrooge right?" Blake murmured quietly as he watched everyone else collecting their gifts. "It's about a ghost from a time before introducing Ebenezer to his past, present, and future. Are you seeing your past, present, or future here Lara?" he whispered against her ear before going to collect his gift. He hadn't meant to come across so brusque, the last thing he wanted to do was hurt her, but she needed to see that maybe it was time to move on and stop living in her past.

"What's going on between you two?" Sylvie asked, handing over Blake's gift as he approached.

"Excuse me?"

"Something is going on between you two. Lara has been

like a premenstrual grizzly bear for the past few days, and now I see why. I thought I was in Narnia when I looked over at you both. The air around you was definitely Arctic."

Blake rolled his eyes. "Sylvie, I don't know what you're talking about. She... I... we-"

"Oh, don't pull that crap with me, Snowden" she growled low enough that no one heard. "I'm not stupid. I've been watching you two. You start showing up in her office, and she's happy. You stop showing up in her office, and she's miserable. Now, of course, I could be reading in to things too deeply and be way off mark, but I don't think I am. Whatever shit has gone down between the two of you, you need to sort it out. She deserves some happiness in her life."

Blake didn't know what to say. Was Lara hurting as much as he was?

"Sylvie, it's not like that. It's not as simple as *sorting it out*." He wished it was.

"Sure it is," she fumed and grabbed a small wrapped box off the large oak table. "Talk to her, take her out, ask her to marry you. I don't know. Just sort this shit out, Blake. I want to see her smiling again after Christmas." And with that, she stomped off towards a group of guys from finance. They were all laughing hysterically and pointing at William Bevin who, for the first time ever, looked embarrassed. He wondered what the joke was all about.

"That's all I want too," he said to nobody, as his gaze travelled to the brunette beauty standing in the corner, nibbling on her thumb nail, watching him nervously.

"What was that all about?" Lara asked when he re-joined her in the corner a moment later.

"Sylvie was just being Sylvie. She makes a good point though."

"She does?"

He nodded. "Yep. Aren't you going to get your gift?" She followed his gaze over to the small amount of unclaimed gifts left on the table.

Turning toward him, she smiled sheepishly. "I don't know if I dare. What if it's from someone I've pissed off? It might be horrendous, and then I'll have to pretend it is the best gift in the world. Maybe I should wait to the end when most people have gone. Then I can grab it and run."

Blake chuckled. It felt so good to see her lightness return, even if it was only for a minute. "You won't know unless you open it. It might be amazing."

"It might not." But she conceded defeat, and marched over to the table.

Blake watched as Lara lifted her gift and spent a moment studying it, obviously looking for any hint of who it might have come from. He'd covered the problem of giving himself away through his writing by asking Caitlyn to write out the gift tag for him. Even at the age of twelve, she had neat, grown up writing. Finally, Lara began tentatively pulling off the silver wrapping paper with frosted white snowflakes. He'd chosen it specifically. It had reminded him of their time playing and laughing together in the park.

Sylvie joined Lara as she pulled her gift from the paper. He'd thought long and hard about what to get her but hadn't been able to decide on just one thing. In the end, he'd got her a simple white china mug decorated with a snowy winter scene and the words 'Hot cocoa was made for days like these' printed in elegant scroll across it. There was also a second wrapped gift that held a voucher for a high end department store so she could buy herself a nice new warm winter coat, decadent hot chocolate sachets, a bottle of the fragrance she wore – it had taken him a long time to work out which one it was—as well as a few other items that he thought she would like. That present was waiting for her back in her office. There were twelve things in total, and he hoped that as a whole they would all form the perfect gift for her. Whether she discovered they were from him or not, he didn't mind, although his initial motive had been for her to do so. He'd wanted to use it as his way of getting to know her and show her the real Blake Snowden. Now he just hoped the gifts would make her smile.

Lara held the mug and said something to Sylvie. They both looked around the room as if trying to work out who the mug was from. Lara and Sylvie continued chatting until their gazes landed on the guys from IT. "It has to be." Sylvie shrieked and clapped her hands together excitedly.

Blake watched as both ladies walked over to the pack of men. Lara stood in front of Jason Miller and smiled coyly at him as she spoke. He said something in return. She held up the mug and Jason simply shrugged with a grin on his face. Blake had seen enough. Lara had not seen the symbolism of the gift and had assumed it was from someone else. That someone else was obviously more than happy to take the credit when he had a beautiful lady standing in front of him.

As he strolled back to his office Blake decided it was time to let his infatuation go and forget about Lara Hollywell. He realised he was chasing an unrealistic dream. She was stuck in the past, and he wanted a bright future.

He dropped his unopened gift by his briefcase on the cabinet in his office and decided to pack up some work. He'd leave early and work from home, away from Lara. At least work was something he was good at.

Chapter Nine

JASON WAS TALKING but Lara wasn't listening. She had just seen Blake walk out without opening his gift and with not so much as a backward glance. He'd looked his usual controlled and powerful self, but there had been something in his posture that didn't sit well with her. He'd looked kind of resigned, sad.

She'd been thinking about Blake all week and then his comments this afternoon about the ghost of Christmas past kept coming back to haunt her. He was right. She was still living with Devin's ghost looming over her. Yet even in her dreams he was telling her to move on. She had been about to look to her future and tell Blake she would love to go to dinner with him, but he'd disappeared.

You've lost your chance, Lara. He wasn't going to hang around indefinitely and wait for you to sort your shit out.

"How about it, Lara? You, me, and a tin of whipped cream, it'll be great."

"Sorry, what?" Lara stepped back, horrified when Jason started skimming his fingers along her collar bone, moving downward.

He stepped in again, crowding her against one of the high-backed chairs. "How about we go back to my place and have some fun?"

Lara gulped and stared at Jason. Was he for real? "I... er... um..."

"Lara!"

She sidestepped Jason and darted across the room to where Sylvie stood. "Oh thank you, thank you, thank you. That was getting a little..."

"Awkward?"

"Yep."

Sylvie glared at Jason. "Want me to go and kick his sexual-harassment-claim arse?" She nodded in the direction of Jason who was now leering at the leggy blond receptionist.

"That won't be necessary. Thanks though."

"Anytime."

As they walked back toward Lara's office, Sylvie wrapped an arm around her shoulder. "What's the deal with you and Blake? He left looking like someone had just shot his puppy."

"There is no deal between Blake and me." Her face dropped. "Maybe there could have been, but I think I royally screwed up any chance with him when I turned him down."

They continued on to Lara's office with Sylvie telling her it wasn't too late, she just needed the courage to go to Blake and tell him the truth of her feelings.

As they entered Lara's office, Sylvie squealed and ran over to a box wrapped in the same paper as Lara's Secret Santa gift.

Lara took the gift from Sylvie with a confused look on her face. "But I've already received my gift."

"Looks like someone wanted to spoil you then doesn't it?" Sylvie gleefully skipped out of the office, obviously ready to get her things together and start her festive break.

Lara sat at her desk, alone, and stared at her new gift. She didn't have it in her to open it right then. Closing down her computer, she decided to call it a day. It was their last working day before the company shut down for the Christmas break after all. On her way out, she would poke her head into Blake's office to wish him and his family a Merry Christmas and test the waters.

She slipped the new gift in to her bag along with some papers she wanted to look over and grabbed her coat as she walked out the door.

"Merry Christmas, boss. I hope you get everything, or rather everyone that you want from Santa." Sylvie smirked as Lara locked her office.

"I don't know what to say to that," Lara replied. "Merry Christmas, Sylvie."

Sylvie's laugh echoed along the hallway as Lara approached Blake's office. She didn't have a clue what she would say to him, but she knew she needed to see him again and hoped he was receptive to seeing her.

Her hopes were dashed when she reached his door and saw, through the small glass windows edging it, that Blake had gone. His lights were off and the door was locked. She sighed, resigned to the fact that maybe things weren't meant to be between them. She would go and spend the Christmas break with her family and try not to think about everything until the new year.

"Do I need to buy a hat?"

That was the greeting Lara received when she opened the door to an unexpected Nan on Christmas Eve.

"Good morning, Nan, and I'm sorry, but what are you talking about? Why would you need a hat? You only just bought your new woollen one this winter." Lara was confused by the surprise visit and Nan's random statement.

Nan brushed past her and walked into the kitchen. "Weddings usually involve a posh frock and a new hat. I need to know if I should be looking for a hat."

Without thinking, Lara started preparing tea for her grandmother. "Why, who's getting married?"

"You are."

"What?" Lara spun around sending teacups crashing onto the worktop. "Who said that?"

Her grandmother draped her coat over the back of a chair and began smoothing out the creases.

"Nan, who told you I'm getting married?"

Nan smiled brightly and joined Lara at the counter. "Daisy and her delightful new friend said you have a boyfriend, her friend's uncle, and you two will probably end up getting married because he loves you."

Lara stumbled back against the fridge. She knew it was only romanticised words from a naïve twelve year old, but still, *love and marriage*? Blake had obviously given up on her, so he certainly didn't love her. She'd had no contact from him since their somewhat awkward conversion in the boardroom the day before.

"They got it wrong, Nan. Blake and I are just work colleagues. We happened to be at the rink at the same time and enjoyed an afternoon together with the girls. It was nothing more, we just wanted the girls to have a good time."

"Uh huh." Nan stepped back over to her coat.

"What's that, that uh huh thing? And what are you doing, you just got here?" Nan was putting her coat back on.

"Get your coat on, Lara. We need to go for a walk."

"What!? Are you crazy? It's freezing out there, and we haven't had tea yet."

"Lara, your old grandmother would like to go for a walk in the snow covered park. I don't know how many more times I will be able to enjoy the snowy peace out there, so indulge me, please."

Nan always knew the correct way to guilt her family into bowing to her needs. Lara threw the tea towel she was holding down and followed. "This is crazy, Nan," she grumbled, even as she pulled on her boots and grabbed her too thin trench coat and Blake's scarf.

"Nice scarf," Nan smirked, as she walked out the door into the frigid air.

"Isn't this nice," Nan commented as she strolled around the park with her arm wrapped through Lara's. A thin pathway around the perimeter had been cleared of snow, ensuring they were able to walk without fear of slipping over. At Nan's ripe old age, it was a constant fear of Lara's that her grandmother would fall one day and not be able to get back up. Of course, she then remembered, Nan still religiously went to the community centre every Thursday afternoon for the senior's yoga session and was probably fitter than Lara herself. Apparently Nan was sweet on old Mr. Tucker, who, by all accounts, was just as fit and lively as Nan was.

"It's great, Nan, but I'm bloody freezing. Can we go back for that tea now, please?" She shivered and rubbed her hands together to warm them slightly.

"Not yet," Nan replied distractedly as she looked around the almost deserted park.

"Nan, we're both going to get ill at this rate, and I don't fancy spending Christmas in the hospital being treated for hypothermia."

"Soon, Lara dear. I'll go back soon. And you need a warmer coat."

Lara's attention was diverted from her nan's use of 'I'll' by a loud whistle. "Boss, come here boy. Not too far."

I know that voice.

Lara turned just as a large German shepherd ran up to Blake who was stood several feet along the path. The dog dropped a red ball at his feet and eagerly wagged its tail, waiting for it to be thrown again.

Her eyes widened. "Nan, did you know Blake was going to be here?" she asked suspiciously.

"Who? How would I know that a very handsome young man with a sexy tush and his dog would be here?" She carried on walking, staring ahead, but Lara could see the laughter in Nan's eyes.

"Nan, you can't just-"

The older woman stopped abruptly and spun to face Lara. With her hands on her hips, Nan said, "Now listen here, little missy. I am sick of seeing you waste your life pining over someone who is never coming back. We've been through this a million times. No more. That young man there," she pointed toward Blake, "is so obviously in love with you, and I know, despite your reluctance to let Devin go, that you like him too. Stop living in the past and go grab your future."

Lara stood, shocked, blinking at her grandmother.

"And while you go and say hello to your future, I'm going to go and say hello to mine." Lara's gaze followed as her nan turned and waved to an elderly gentleman standing at the gate on the far side of the park. He waved back with a huge grin on his face. "Don't worry what time you make it around tomorrow," she said. And then, with a wink, Nan shuffled off to meet her gentleman friend.

Lara turned back toward where Blake was standing. He threw the ball once again and when he turned their eyes met. At first, he seemed surprised by her presence, his eyes widening in shock. Then his lips curled deliciously into a broad grin that had her heart fluttering. As if being pulled by a magnet, Lara began walking toward Blake. The dog dropped the ball again and barked excitedly. Blake threw it, putting extra effort into getting the ball a fair distance across the snow covered park. The dog bounded off and Blake turned to walk toward Lara.

They met under a large oak tree and Blake instinctively removed his jacket, draping it over Lara's shoulders.

"Lara? What are you doing out here all by yourself? You'll catch your death."

Blake's jacket felt wonderful, not only because it still held his heat and warmed her instantly, but because it smelled of him, felt like him, was him. It felt warm and cosy and… like home.

She pulled the jacket around her and mumbled her thanks before explaining why she was there.

"We were set up," Blake laughed. "I mentioned to my sister that I needed to take Boss for a walk, and she said we couldn't go to our usual place, which was closed. She said I needed to bring him here and at this time." He shook his head in exasperation.

Boss ran up to them and dropped the ball at Lara's feet. She smiled down at him and scratched his ears. "I didn't know you had a dog."

Blake threw the ball and Boss chased after it through the snow. "It never came up." He shrugged. "Some things never came up."

They continued walking for a while, discussing the underhanded ploys of their families and what their plans were for Christmas day.

When they reached the main gate, Blake grabbed Lara's hands and turned her to face him. "Lara, look, I need to talk to you about something and I'm freezing my nuts off out here. Would you come back to my place and join me for something to eat?"

She didn't think, didn't second guess, she went with

her gut. "I'd love to."

"Come in. Make yourself at home." Blake opened the front door to his rather impressive, detached home and gestured Lara inside. He lived about ten minutes out of town in an area known for its affluence. The house itself, although not overly large, was beautifully decorated with a mix of contemporary colours and a few antique pieces of furniture. He took her coat and hung it in a closet while she looked at the few pieces of artwork hung on the hallway walls.

They ventured into the living room and Lara gaped in awe. She had always taken Blake for a typical carefree bachelor. The overly Christmassy room in front of her did not match her assumptions about him at all. In the corner stood a huge Christmas tree decorated with hundreds of intricate ornaments and baubles. The tree must have stood at least eight feet tall, and the lights alone were enough to illuminate the room with a gentle glow. Hanging over the fireplace was a garland decorated with berries and pine cones that gave the room a beautiful aroma. Other, more subtle Christmas touches strategically placed here and there ensured the room oozed Christmas spirit without being over the top.

"Blake, this is beautiful," Lara murmured.

He looked around as if seeing it for the first time. "I guess."

"You guess? You must have known what you were doing when you were putting it all up." She carefully lifted a silver and ice-blue photo frame that contained a picture of a man who appeared to be a few years older than Blake. With features so similar to Blake's she knew he must have been one of Blake's older brothers. Also in the photo were a stunning blonde lady and two children, one boy and one girl - Caitlyn.

Blake laughed. "As much as I would like to, I can't take credit for all of this. With two sisters-in-law, three nieces, and two nephews who all adore Christmas, there isn't a hope in hell of me getting away with no decorations. They always come around and do it for me, I just foot the bill." Lara looked around again. Yes, there was definitely a female touch to the decorations.

Suddenly, there was a loud howl from somewhere in the house that caused Lara to jump and almost drop the frame. Blake just laughed and shook his head as he left the room. "I guess Boss wants his dinner first."

Lara was looking at more family photos on the wall when she heard a scratching noise followed by rapid tapping. "Boss, get your arse back in here," Blake hollered before his large and energetic dog came bounding into the room, his legs almost giving way as they skidded on the wooden flooring. Blake came running in just as the dog jumped up on Lara, pinning her shocked body against the wall as he licked her face.

"Boss, down boy," Blake yelled again, dragging the dog away by his collar.

"Sorry," Blake said looking up at Lara whilst trying to get Boss to sit. "He gets a bit excited when I have visitors." He crouched down in front of the dog. "Are you going to behave, boy, and welcome Lara to our home nicely?" Boss panted and wagged his tail again. "Okay then. Good boy."

"I've got to ask," she said. "Why the name Boss?"

Blake laughed. "Isn't it obvious? He thinks he's the boss around here. It's a running joke in the family that I'm out-bossed by a smelly mutt." He patted his dog's head. "This boy here has me wrapped right around his paw."

Lara smiled as she watched the way the two interacted with each other. Blake obviously adored his dog as much as Boss adored Blake. She stepped away from the wall and crouched next to Blake to scratch Boss's head. "He's adorable," she said. Boss lapped up the attention for a minute before stretching out on the rug in front of the fireplace and falling asleep.

"Well, I'm pleased to say, you made the cut," Blake joked, smiling down at his dog. "He's not usually so trusting on a first visit. I guess he likes you too."

Lara followed Blake through into the kitchen with his words echoing in her head, *he likes you too.*

Chapter Ten

LARA PLACED HER knife and fork on her empty plate and sat back with a contented sigh. "Blake, that was delicious. Who knew you were anything other than a high flying businessman?"

He chuckled, grabbing his glass of wine. "I've told you before, there is a lot about me you don't know, Lara. I'm a man of many hidden talents."

"Is that a good thing or a bad thing?" she joked.

"That depends on what you think you know." He shrugged.

"What does that mean?"

He sighed. "People have a tendency to pre-judge me based on what I do. They – mostly women – think that because I have some high-powered position that I'm a millionaire playboy just wanting a good time. They want my body and for me to lavish gifts on them. Either that, or they see me as a socially outcast workaholic." He shook his head. "I'm none of those things. I'm just an ordinary guy who has worked his butt off to impress and prove he's worthy. I just want to be successful in whatever I do."

"I don't believe you are any of those things," Lara said softly.

Blake cocked his brows.

"Okay, maybe once I did... you do, after all, have a reputation. But you forget, I'm also in the boardroom with you a lot of the time. I see your passion and dedication. I see the real you then."

"Do you?"

She smiled. "Of course I do. You're hard to miss, Blake."

With their meal finished, Blake told Lara to head back into the living room while he cleared the dishes. Earlier, he had lit a fire, so the room was warm and cosy when she entered. She took a seat on the end of the sofa near the fire, and, without thinking, she pulled her legs up under her and settled in with the remains of her glass of wine. As she stared into the dancing flames of the fire, she thought back over the events of the afternoon and evening. She wanted to be mad at her grandmother for being so underhand, but all she could do was smile at the extremes she had gone to so Lara would be happy.

She then thought about Blake. She'd thought she

knew him, but she was beginning to see that maybe he was right. She'd only known *of* Blake. She knew how hard he worked, how ruthless he was to make sure things got done. But she didn't know him on a deeper, more intimate level. There were hints, aspects of the real him that she had picked up on, but there was still so much to learn about him. She thought back over all of the fantasies she'd had of him over the years and realised they weren't all hormone driven and purely about his fine physical appearance. She had indeed seen glimpses of the real Blake Snowden, but now she wanted to see and know more. So much more.

Boss came over and rested his head in her lap. She scratched his ears and a sudden jolt of emotion swept through her. She felt as though she were living in the quintessential Christmas card image. The perfect family home complete with roaring fire, dog, and presents surrounding the tree. She felt cosy, as though she were home. It was in that moment that Lara realised how lonely her own home had become, and she looked again, trying to soak the feeling in.

She hadn't noticed the fact that Blake was stood leaning against the doorway watching her. Their gazes locked and she felt her cheeks flush. He was staring at her with an expression of lust and devotion. With her mind racing, she wasn't sure what her face was showing, but she didn't want him to stop looking at her that way.

Blake pushed away from the door frame and wandered further into the room. "Can I ask you a personal question? You can tell me where to go if you want."

"It depends on what it is." She took a sip of her

wine. She needed a distraction from the way he was looking at her.

"When was your last relationship?"

She ran a hand through Boss's long fur, thinking it through, wondering how honest she should be. "Seven years ago," she whispered.

"Seven years? Wow!" He sounded surprised.

She felt the need to explain further. "After Devin died, I kind of retreated into myself. My world had fallen apart. I didn't know anything beyond what we'd had together. He'd been my life. When we buried him, I thought we'd buried my present and future with him too. I clung on to our past, my memories, like they were my lifeline.

"Eventually, I pulled myself together to concentrate on building a career, and that became my only focus. I wasn't interested in guys. I dated some here and there, but none of them were Devin. None of them could make me laugh like he did or hold and comfort me like he did. None of them could have possibly loved me like he had. If I did find myself even vaguely attracted to someone, I would end things before they became complicated."

"Why would things be complicated?" Blake's brow crinkled with a look of genuine interest mixed with confusion.

"I didn't want to betray Devin. I didn't want to disrespect his memory," she admitted with a slight lift of her shoulders. Lara's eyes met his for a split second before she resumed staring into the fire.

"Lara, I'm sure I'm not the first to say this, but you wouldn't be betraying him," he said softly. "You deserve to be happy. He'd want you to be happy."

She nodded as a lone tear trickled down her cheek. "I know he would, but it's hard, Blake. When you have a whole life mapped out and it's all ripped away from you in the blink of an eye, you're left in limbo. You don't know which path to take or what is the right or wrong thing to do. You become immune to living."

Blake was by her side before she could suck in another shuddering breath. He pulled her into his arms and stroked his fingers through her hair. "There was no right or wrong thing to do. The man you loved was cruelly taken from you. But you didn't die with him, Lara. You are still very much alive and you deserve to be happy. You deserve everything."

He held onto her for several minutes in silence. For the first time in a long time, she felt comfort from someone's embrace.

"I need to be honest with you," he said eventually, speaking softly into her hair. "I deliberately got tickets and bribed Caitlyn to go ice skating with me that day. I needed to see you again. I like you, Lara. Like, *really* like you. I want to take you out again, show you things and places. And I'm hoping you might feel the same because, in an ideal world, I would really like to see where things could go with us."

She closed her eyes. "I'm not sure I can, Blake."

He pulled her closer. "I know you're reluctant to let go, I understand that. You can set the pace, Lara. We'll take things as fast or as slowly as you want. I just want to be here for you, get to know you. And, when you're ready, I would love for you to give us a try."

You have to let go, Lara. It's time to be happy. Devin's whispered words from so many of her recent dreams replayed in Lara's mind. All of them – Mum, Nan,

Debbie, Heidi – they had all been telling her for years that it was time to let go and find happiness.

When she re-opened her eyes, it was with a new found clarity. She'd had feelings for Blake for a very long time, but her own self-imposed love exile had pushed the thoughts of him ever becoming more than her fantasy away. Yet there he was, declaring that he cared about and wanted her.

"Okay," she whispered.

"Okay?"

"Okay, I'm ready. I want to get to know you too. I want to laugh with you, and fight with you, and even dance with you. I just want to be happy again, Blake. But we need to take it slow."

He pulled her to her feet and wrapped her in his arms. Shifting their bodies from leg to leg he turned them gently, as if to unheard music. "I can do slow. Do you know how happy this makes me?" Lifting her chin, he leaned in and covered her lips with his. It was a tentative kiss at first, a gentle touching of lips that told Lara so much about how Blake was feeling. The longer she stayed in his kiss, the more pressure he applied. He was allowing her to control the pace and it meant everything to her.

Eventually, Lara wrapped her arms around Blake and encouraged him to deepen the kiss even further. He was soon lightly tracing his tongue along her bottom lip, and she was opening for him. He delved in, tickling her tongue with his and pushing harder with his lips. As her heartbeat raced and their mingled breaths became deeper, Blake's movements grew more heated. When he kissed his way along her cheek and down her jawline to her neck, Lara threw her head back and silently said goodbye to Devin. It was time to let him go and move on with her life.

Life felt pretty damn great for Blake. Having kissed Lara relentlessly for what felt like hours, he'd eventually pulled her down onto the sofa and simply cuddled her. He'd wanted to take things further, had wanted to claim her in the most primal way possible, but he knew – or hoped – that would happen eventually. What Lara needed now was time. So they'd curled up on the sofa with Blake cuddling her from behind and Lara reaching out to scratch Boss's head as they stared into the fire.

When he'd watched her from the doorway it had been like watching a movie clip of his future in crystal clear, pure high definition. He'd wanted to reach out and grasp the vision. He'd wanted Lara, and for the first time, he felt like he might actually be able to get her.

Then, hearing her admit she was still very much in love with her dead fiancé, he felt once again that maybe she was unreachable. That thought had been like a stab in the heart. Blake knew it was a cliché, but when something felt so real, so right, he knew he had to fight for it. If he didn't, he would always regret not knowing what could have been. So he had told her everything he felt.

When she'd said she was ready to move on, he'd almost dropped down on one knee right there and then. Almost.

"Blake?" Lara asked tentatively.

"Yeah?"

"If we do this, see where things go, what happens at work? You know, with us?"

He lifted onto his elbow and looked down at her. "Nothing happens at work. You're still you, and I'm still me. We've both worked hard to get where we are, nobody is going to think anything untoward is going on because we're together."

She didn't look convinced. "Lara, listen to me," he continued. "The company isn't like that, not unless something underhand is going on. Besides, what happens in our personal lives is our business. It has nothing to do with anybody but us."

She shuffled back into him and sighed. "I hope you're right."

He kissed her hair. "I know I'm right."

The old grandfather clock in the corner striking twelve roused Blake from the sleep he'd fallen into. As his eyes sprung open, he was immediately greeted by the most beautiful sight in the world. Lara was curled up next to him with her head on his chest. Her hair was splayed out around her, so he reached out to gently run his fingers through its softness, hoping he wouldn't disturb her. The whole scene was a feast for his senses, and he wanted to take it all in, wanted to memorise it all in case the dream was ripped from him.

Lara stirred and peered up at him. "Hi," she said shyly.

"Hi back. Merry Christmas, Lara." He pecked her lips with a soft kiss.

She peered at the clock and her eyes widened. "Wow, we fell asleep huh?" He grinned and nodded. "Well, Merry Christmas then, I guess." Her eyes sparkled with her radiant smile.

He was tempted to kiss her again, but seeing as it was officially Christmas day, he wanted to do something first. Lara grumbled as Blake shifted her back slightly and went to get something from under the tree.

"It looks like Santa's been," he said as he handed her a box she recognised.

"You brought that here?" She took the box wrapped in silver paper with frosted snowflakes from him. "Why?"

Blake lifted a gift wrapped in gold paper with a red ribbon from under the tree as well. "Recognise this?"

Lara gasped. "That's my gift to you." She then slapped a hand over her mouth as she realised her error.

Blake chuckled. "I knew it all along. I wanted to be your Secret Santa, Lara. I wanted the chance to buy you a gift without seeming too creepy. I'd hoped you might work out it was from me and... oh, I don't know, it seemed like a good idea at the time."

Lara stroked his flushed cheeks. "You rigged it?" He nodded.

"Oh my God, Blake, do you know how difficult it is to buy the perfect gift for you?" she squeaked, as she playfully punched his arm. "I didn't know what to get you. I bet you hate it."

Blake dropped the gift-wrapped box and gently pushed Lara so she was lying back once again. With his body braced over hers, he smiled down and stared into her eyes. "It doesn't matter what it is. There could be a lump of coal in there for all I care. All I want is you, Lara. You've given me all I need, all I could possibly ask for." He pulled her hand to his chest, resting it over his heart. "You, my love, are my perfect gift."

About The Author

E.J. Shortall was born and raised in London, England where she currently still lives with her teenage son.

Having worked in education for the better part of twelve years, EJ decided a change was needed and, following a moment of inspiration, she decided to put pen to paper and start writing her first novel, Silver Lining. Not content with just the one, she continued with book two and hopes to write many more.

She has always enjoyed reading, but found it was mostly just a holiday extravagance. Then she discovered a certain worldwide best seller, and that was it she was hooked. Reading quickly became an obsession and she couldn't devour books fast enough. The books on her shelves and reading device range from sweet, Young Adult romances, to smouldering erotic encounters.

Aside from reading and writing, EJ also enjoys amateur photography and cake decorating.

"I am on one amazing roller coaster ride at the moment, meeting new and wonderful people, discovering new music gems to integrate into my stories, and learning so many new skills. I can't wait to see where this journey takes me."

To find out more about E.J. and her other titles, visit her:

Email:
ejshortallauthor@gmail.com

Website:
www.ejshortallauthor.com

Facebook:
www.facebook.com/e.j.shortallauthor

Twitter:
@EJShortall

Also by
E. J. Shortall

Silver Lining (Silver series book one)

Amber Merchant had it all. Living with and engaged to her teenage sweetheart, a nice house and the job of her dreams. Not anymore!

Following a devastating revelation from her Fiancé, Amber finds herself single once again and moving on. To protect herself she vows to stay away from men and guard her wounded heart.

During an evening out to celebrate her newly single life, a chance encounter with a tall, dark and handsome stranger leaves Amber's head reeling. Intrigued by her draw to him but scared for her heart she flees.

Craig Silver, twenty nine year old CEO, is the last person Amber needs in her life. Battling his own demons, Craig is content on a life of meaningless affairs, one night stands and no commitments.

At first it seems their attraction is mutual… until she runs.

When fate intervenes and their paths cross again, Craig refuses to take no for an answer. Encouraging Amber to take a chance on a single date he sets them on a path of love, lust, truth and deception.

Silver Dove (Silver series book two)

Full of romance, intrigue, emotion and passion, Silver Dove is the concluding part to Craig and Amber's story that began in Silver Lining.

After the chaos of their early relationship and with their history of broken pasts behind them, Craig and Amber prepare to say 'I Do' on their Happy Ever After.

Life rarely runs to plan though.

Amber has fought long and hard to bury her fears and become a stronger person, but when old feelings resurface and tragedy strikes, it takes an intervention from Craig to prove her doubts are unfounded and to believe in love and hope.

Just when they think they are at a point where they can be happy and move forward together, the pair find themselves fighting obstacles and difficulties that will truly test the strength of their bond.

Can Amber gather the strength to fight against the forces trying to destroy her? Will Craig keep his promises of remaining truthful? As a couple are they tough enough to battle through these turbulent times and emerge stronger than ever?

Prepared to Fight

Live each day as if it were your last. Worry only about yourself. Work hard and never, ever fall in love. That's Olivia Buchanan's motto and she stands by it every day.

Feisty, headstrong and confident, recent graduate Liv is fighting to succeed in the male dominated field she has chosen as her career. As an architect for her best friend's father's respected London based company, her chance to shine and become recognised comes when she lands the prestigious account for GO Sports and Leisure.

Armed with her plans and determination, Liv is ready to deliver the presentation of her life. That is, until he walks in. The mysterious personal trainer from the gym. The only man to have ever made her heart flutter. But he isn't all he seems.

When MMA fighter, Nathan Oakes offers Liv a business proposition to join him in Southern France, she's left questioning his motives and wonders if she should refuse. She's also equally intrigued by the prospect of what the trip could do for her career.

Liv has no time for a relationship. Nate doesn't want one. When forced to live side by side, though, feelings are stretched and emotions are battled. Can they keep their professional and personal lives separate and prevent them both from falling into something they need to avoid? Are they prepared to fight?